## *It was in that bed that she now dreamed.*

As stiff and spare as she was in real life, in her dreams she had become lush and desirable. She knew with some cynicism that it had to be a dream, because no man alive had ever affected her as did the phantom in her thoughts.

Did other women experience such dreams? Why were they happening to her now?

It was irritating to dream that way. She spent many nights trying to get the phantom to show his face. He never did—until one night....

That night the phantom sat naked at her bedside. His gorgeous body was shadowed by the lacy canopy, and the dusty hair that covered him invited her touch. His muscles bunched as he turned to her. Her eyes strained anxiously, and she saw his face.

Her phantom lover was John Peal.

# MEN at WORK

➤—MILLIONAIRE'S CLUB   ⬚—BOARDROOM BOYS   ⬚—MAGNIFICENT MEN
⬚—TALL, DARK & SMART   ⬚—DOCTOR, DOCTOR   ⬚—MEN OF THE WEST
ᛉᛏᛉ—MEN OF STEEL   ⬚—MEN IN UNIFORM

# MEN at WORK
# LASS SMALL
# AN IRRITATING MAN

TALL, DARK
AND SMART

E=MC²

*Silhouette Books*

Published by Silhouette Books

America's Publisher of Contemporary Romance

SILHOUETTE BOOKS
300 East 42nd St.,
New York, N.Y. 10017

ISBN 0-373-81015-6

AN IRRITATING MAN

This edition published by arrangement with Harlequin Books S.A.

® and TM are trademarks of Harlequin Books S.A., used under license. Trademarks indicated with ® are registered in the United States Patent and Trademark Office, the Canadian Trade Marks Office and in other countries.

**Printed in U.S.A.**

Dear Reader,

Good title. Now, who would chide me for saying men can be irritating? They are so charming and they can do just about anything and reach higher and solve things. They are remarkable. They don't always understand tears. They forget important occasions. They are also irritating.

But they are charming and humorous. They can be so gentle and supportive. They can stand and just look at someone who is being obnoxious. It is a deadly look. This is the same man who can kiss a woman's finger when she has a cut. Who can hug a woman who is at the end of her rope and is crying.

Men are worth the effort.

With my love,

*Lass*

Please address questions and book requests to:
Silhouette Reader Service
U.S.: 3010 Walden Ave., P.O. Box 1325, Buffalo, NY 14269
Canadian: P.O. Box 609, Fort Erie, Ont. L2A 5X3

# Chapter One

It was September when John Peal came home to Tarkington, there in the lower middle part of Indiana, and the town was astonished that he'd returned to them. He apparently intended to stay, or at least be there for a time.

John had quite a name by then. His last book had been made into a major motion picture, and John himself had made the gossip columns as he cut a swath through hordes of beautiful women who wore indiscreet clothing.

One article had particularly irritated Talullah Metcalf, Tarkington spinster, school teacher and cat lover. Talullah had been half orphaned as a child and raised by a reluctant spinster great aunt in her paternal grandparents' home, where she still lived.

She was a year and a half younger than John Peal's thirty-one years, but she was an old maid, while the article implied he was a swashbuckling rake. It rankled. John Peal, of little old Tarkington, Indiana, was riding high.

Why had he come back?

Just last month her neighbor's grandson, Paul Morrison, had been in California on business. Paul was only twenty-five, too young to be an old Tarkington chum, but he had phoned John Peal, out there in Los Angeles, and John had moved Paul into his condo and treated him like a brother.

He'd taken Paul everywhere, shared the beautiful, carelessly dressed women, and Paul thought he'd glimpsed Paradise. It was a wonder John had ever gotten rid of Paul.

Actually, it had been Paul who'd left. His vacation time had run out, and he'd wanted to get back to his job. That just proved that Paul Morrison had no use for such fakery and was more mature than John Peal.

"Too rich for my blood," Paul had reported to Talullah with a grin. "Man, what a life! I don't know how John survives! He asked how many kids you had by now, Talullah. He thought you'd married Pete. It really surprised him that you'd never married."

"Pete? That was years ago."

"I told John that." Paul studied her for a minute. Her sleek body, her brown eyes, her tightly bunned, brown hair. "He couldn't believe you weren't married."

"I was born an old maid."

Paul didn't disagree. "He's a very nice man, Talullah. Most of what you read is hype. The women want to be seen, and John is nice to be seen with. He has a good solid name now, but he hasn't changed. Women know they're safe with him."

"With John?"

Paul's laugh was filled with genuine humor. "It's very interesting to see some gorgeous dolly sitting next to him and listening to him talk about...other things." Paul looked at Talullah assessingly, because John had talked about *her.* "And he listens to them. They really love him. So do the men. He's rare."

Even Linda Redburn called from Washington State. Linda and Talullah had been best friends all their lives, even through college; then Mark Redburn had taken her away with him clear out to Seattle, Washington. Talullah had told Linda she wasn't a very loyal friend to choose Mark over friendship. Linda thought that was hilarious. So did Mark. Talullah still missed Linda after all those years.

When Linda called she exclaimed, "Hey, John Peal is moving back to Tarkington!"

"We've heard." Talullah's voice was sour.

"To little old Tarkington, Indiana!"

"There's even going to be a *reception* for him!" And she waited to hear Linda hoot.

"Blast, I wish we could be there. It'll be such fun! Give John my love."

Of course his coming home was in all the papers. The Indianapolis *Star* talked about the native son and his return to his roots. And everyone made such a fuss over him! It was all so ridiculous that Talullah had to become quite parsimonious just to show that not everyone was so silly. All that fuss over John Peal.

His books were good. Well written, insightful, stirring, satisfying. Talullah had never admitted to anyone that she read John's books. She didn't buy them in Tarkington. She bought them in the Castleton Mall down in Indianapolis, and she read them avidly, looking for flaws, ready to sneer. But he could write.

He was also irritatingly good-looking. And he had the bluest eyes. It wasn't that he was so handsome; it was something about his manner, the way he stood and how he handled himself. A strength. A presence. Even as a teenager his voice had been deep, calm, as if he were in charge. Very annoying.

Just seeing him on the pages of *People* or *Time* or *USA Today,* or on *Entertainment Tonight,* was astonishing. The women with him didn't even look at the camera, they were all looking up at John. Women could be very silly.

She would never be that way. Talullah was sure of that. John Peal was just a plain, ordinary, Tarkington Peal. And the town was having a reception for him! She couldn't get over that.

When the Nolans had come back to live in Tarkington, after ten years in Michigan, they didn't get a reception. And there had been five of them. But just John Peal was going to have a reception.

Would he bring a woman with him? Everyone knew how those people on the West Coast lived. Would he do that to Pastor Fredericks? He was probably depraved and had come to Tarkington to kick a cocaine addiction. Or maybe he had agreed to be the Midwest distributor? How would Police Chief George Townsend handle that?

Talullah did go to the reception. If she hadn't, it would have looked strange, as if she were avoiding him or something. She changed her dress five times in thirty minutes and almost cried. Why would she cry? It was just that nothing looked right on her. Why did she have to look nice? By any chance was she trying to compete with those almost-dressed females who'd clung to him? Of course not!

Everyone in town was there, along with quite a few people from surrounding towns who had no business horning in on a Tarkington celebration. Celebration? Why should Tarkington celebrate just because John Peal was back in town?

She sipped punch and tried to pretend not to be interested. She talked to the old ladies who were standing around because she knew the time would come when she would be an old lady standing around at receptions and she would want someone to talk to her. It was bread cast upon the waters, she told herself, but she really did it so she wouldn't have to look at John Peal.

He was there in the same room, and his laugh was as delightful to her ears as it had always been. And the press of people around him was the same. Apparently his laugh and his charm had survived his disgraceful drug-ridden West Coast orgy.

He was probably yellow-skinned from hepatitis and wore makeup to conceal his dissipations. She thoughtfully munched the goodies the Book Club had prepared. *The Portrait of Dorian Gray* came to mind. It was too bad John couldn't do that, too. Keep a portrait in the attic that looked as he actually should, while his wholesome body continued on like an innocent man's.

"Hello, Talullah." He was right at her elbow. Because of the crowd he had to stand very close, and his sweet breath was on her cheek!

With unfocused eyes she looked up and replied, "Urp."

He smiled and said, "It's good to see you...." His strong fingers closed gently on her arm.

Then some vulgar attention-getter said, "Look over here, John!" And Talullah wasn't blinded by the flashbulb because she was looking up at John.

He was healthy. He looked hale and hearty and in good shape. He might very well have a rotting portrait in his attic. He looked as he always had: devastating. How awful. While she stared, others came between them. Distractedly he tried to talk to her, but people horned in, and she was separated from him. She continued to stare, and impatiently he looked in her direction several times, searching for her. She left right after that.

She saw a copy of the picture in the *Star,* and she could have died. Other than the fact that she was fully clothed and that her face without makeup looked like a washed-out blob, she was exactly like all the other women in pictures with John. She looked as if she were searching for the moon, and the moon was John Peal. How humiliating.

Thank God she was a teacher. At least the kids didn't constantly talk about John Peal. She had lesson plans, distracting children, and all sorts of things she could think about besides John Peal, writer, who had returned to his roots and was being lionized.

How long would it be, she wondered, before there was some *other* subject to discuss when two people met in Tarkington?

The Metcalf house was on the opposite side of town from the house John Peal rented. Her grandparents' house had been in the family for more than a hundred years. It needed new plumbing again, and the electricity was eccentric. The kitchen was impossible. But the porches were wide, the rooms big, and the furniture treasured.

He came to see her. He simply dropped in just like a plain, ordinary, everyday person. She'd had no idea he would come by her house, and she had on scruffies! She looked simply ghastly. She blushed and said, "Uh, hello...uh, John." And she blushed even worse.

He smiled and said, "It's nice to be back." He appeared to be very comfortable with her.

She was a wreck. "Why did you come to Tarkington?" Her tone sounded almost accusatory! And how many times had he been asked that same inane question?

"It's home."

"You haven't really lived here since high-school days. You were away at college when your dad took that job with GE and moved to New York."

"I'm a Tarkingtonian to the core. This is my home, my native land, and I'm going to live here and be part of this place."

"I can't see how Tarkington could interest you after the way you've lived."

"Could I sit down?"

They were still standing in the entrance hall. "Oh. Uh. Yes, of course." She gestured vaguely.

He strolled into her living room just as her grandmother came in from the kitchen. "John!" she exclaimed. "How nice to see you, dear."

"Hello, Mrs. Metcalf." He leaned down to the

tiny woman and kissed her cheek. "How are you?"

"Older."

John laughed. "And Mr. Metcalf?"

"Out in the greenhouse making wine. This is a vintage year."

"Still making moonshine, huh? I remember sampling some one year. Almost fried my brain."

"Don't ever say that to him. He thinks his fence-row grapes are nectar-making stuff. He's over eighty, you know, and his taste buds have deteriorated."

"Gram…" Talullah began.

"Did you bring one of your women along?"

"Gram!" Talullah gasped in soft horror as she waited for John's reply.

"Not this time. I thought I'd check out the local talent."

Mrs. Metcalf chuckled. "Rascal. You always were a rascal. Nice to have you home again, John. Come to dinner."

"I'd like to."

"We're having pigs' knuckles and sauerkraut." Such an invitation was meant to flatter John. It was a family meal in the corn and hog oriented Midwest. She smiled, knowing he must be pleased. "I've stewed some of those yellow apples from the tree down by the tennis court."

"Is your tennis court still there?"

"Grown up with weeds. It would be nice if some newcomer would volunteer to skin off the court and roll it nicely."

"Not me." John grinned at her.

"I seem to remember your father was lazy and good-for-nothing, too."

"Only with hellions who try to get free labor."

"I'd bake you a pie or two." Mrs. Metcalf grinned back at John.

"We'll negotiate."

As the conversation continued, Talullah did nothing but gasp and make protesting sounds. She didn't want John there for dinner. She didn't want him underfoot working on the tennis court. She hadn't ironed that week's wash, and she didn't have anything to wear. And they could hardly serve John Peal pigs' knuckles and sauerkraut! Good grief.

"Gram, John doesn't want to eat dinner here tonight. Perhaps another time."

"I haven't had pigs' knuckles and sauerkraut in a year of Tuesdays."

Talullah squinted as she sorted out how long that would be.

Mildred Metcalf smugly tucked in a few stray locks and supplied the answer, "Seven years."

John complained, "The trouble with age is that the mind dulls." And his eyes twinkled with delight.

Mrs. Metcalf sighed. "Talullah *has* aged terribly since you knew her."

"...all those years ago," John added solemnly.

"You deserve pigs' knuckles and sauerkraut," Talullah snapped.

"And, along with Philo's taste buds, Talullah's disposition has deteriorated."

"Really?" John's amused eyes rested on Talullah. "I'm looking forward to the evening. What time should I be here to help set the table?"

"Five-thirty. Philo will permit you to sample some of his wines, and I don't want you to handle the china after that. Don't allow him to force more than three on you. I will not tolerate drunken hilarity at the supper table."

"Yes ma'am," he replied obediently.

"Apply that attitude to the tennis court." Mrs. Metcalf turned away. She was eighty-three. Philo was in fact two years younger.

"I didn't come back to Tarkington to refurbish your tennis court!"

She turned around at the kitchen door. "Why did you come back?"

Talullah listened avidly.

"To write a book about bossy ladies."

"I'll see if I can find you several to study." Mildred raised her chin before she turned away and left the room.

He smiled down at Talullah. "Our grandparents survive well."

She had to agree. "They're the kind who encourage the rest of us in thinking being old is quite nice."

"Being old is like being a teenager: you hear only about the ones who have it tough."

They examined each other rather intently. Then she looked away self-consciously. John said, "I hadn't known you and Pete broke up."

"Our engagement was a mistake. To have married would only have perpetrated the error. He would have been miserable with me."

"I doubt that."

"He was too young."

"He's older than I am."

"He still isn't married."

"You made a lucky escape."

She began to relax. He had always been kind to her. Well, now and then. Like when her dog was hit by that car when she was five. He'd sat on the curb with her while she cried, and he hadn't made any nasty remarks at all.

"Well..." She tried to think of a way to get him to leave so she could iron something to wear.

"It's so...real to be back. I walk around, and it's like everything else was stage settings."

"Europe's like that," she said impulsively. "As if you're walking through picture post cards."

"When did you go?"

"I took a spring break student tour. I got to go free, as a chaperon."

"That must have been jolly."

"It *was* fun. The kids are great. Their ages ranged from fourteen to eighteen, and they were so interested. Most of them had to work all year for the fare. Those under sixteen did yards, garages, attics, snow shoveling, just about anything, so they appreciated the fact that they could go, and they paid attention. Travel really is broadening."

Her cheeks flushed a little. He'd been everywhere—including a nudist beach at the Cannes Film Festival. There'd been a picture of him with a nude girl whose back had been to the camera as she faced John.

He said, "I've never been beyond Europe. I'd like to see the pyramids. India. The Great Wall. I'd like to be a civilian in a shuttle. I have my name in."

"Motion sickness lurks on the edge of my resolve. I'm not sure I could handle space."

"I'll take pictures," John promised, "and give a full report."

"There are those prescription patches for behind the ear. They really work. I suppose I could always try one of those."

He smiled at her, his eyes kind. "Do you still play tennis?"

"Not since the weeds took over the court."

"I might be convinced to help you peel the court. Peals are good peelers." He laughed, a nice, soft, sexy chuckle.

"You're so familiar, and yet you're such a stranger," she said with an earnest frown.

"It won't take long for us to be comfortable again."

"Spoken like a stranger. John, you forget that we *never* got along."

"Why, Talullah, we've been good friends all our lives!"

"You've plagued and baited and antagonized me all my life!"

"I did not either!"

"Children, children!" Mrs. Metcalf sounded amused as she came in with a bouquet of nasturtiums for the small round table in front of the south windows. "At it again?"

"Still," corrected Talullah with a superior look at John. "Her statement proves exactly what I said."

"Grandparents are unreliable witnesses," he shot back. "They tend to be prejudiced and biased."

"Redundant."

Mildred Metcalf turned her head to Talullah. "Grandparents are redundant?" she inquired, knowing full well how the conversation had been going.

"John said prejudiced *and* biased." Then, with her grandmother there to act as John's hostess, Talullah seized the opportunity to escape. "Nice to see you, John, but I must rush. You're really coming for pigs' knuckles and sauerkraut?"

"With relish." He grinned.

"Oh. Well. See you then." She went up the stairs two at a time and vanished.

John and Mrs. Metcalf exchanged a long, communicating look, and Mrs. Metcalf nodded once in satisfaction. She put the nasturtiums on the table and advised, "Wear casual clothes tonight, dear. We're not dressing." Then she smiled. "Don't be discouraged."

"Am I so obvious?"

"I've lived a long time." She went to him and laid her small, wrinkled hand on his chest.

He covered her hand with his own. "I thought she'd married Pete."

"She wanted you to believe she was desirable."

"So to impress me, she was going to marry another man?" His eyes were both amused and scoffing.

"She had to prove to herself that she was attractive." Mrs. Metcalf was firm.

John hesitated. "She didn't know that?"

"She still doesn't."

"My God. What can I do?"

"There is no one else," Mrs. Metcalf declared truthfully. "There never has been. You'll just have to be clever and patient."

"Does she know she loves me?"

"Not a clue."

"With my parents living in New York, and my brothers scattered, and the grandparents permanently moved to Florida, I've had no contact here.

I haven't been back in a long, long time. I was astounded that she wasn't married."

He slid his hands into his pockets and lifted his head back as he looked out a window at the changing fall leaves. He said softly, "Thank God Paul Morrison had the persistence to track me down when he was in California. We didn't even know each other when I lived here. I knew the Morrisons had a kid, but I couldn't remember his name or what he looked like. We had a good time." He grinned at Mrs. Metcalf. "After he said Talullah wasn't married, I tried to give him the whole city."

"He told me how kind you were to him."

"I just assumed all my life that, when we grew up, Talullah and I would get married. It never occurred to me that she didn't realize that simple fact."

"There must have been something lacking in your means of communication." She spaced the words as she shook her head slowly.

"I rewrite a lot."

"The two of you never really dated."

"But we were always in the same group. I always picked her up. I had mono for my senior prom, so I couldn't take her." He still regretted that. "But I got Smoky to take her."

"She had a rotten time, and she cried."

"I felt bad about it, but Smoky was the only guy I could trust with her. I terrified him."

"You were obviously too subtle."

"I'll go up the stairs now, sweep her into my arms and carry her off on my horse."

"Prince died almost…my land, it must be seven years ago."

"I'll borrow a bicycle."

She laughed silently. "Perhaps we can work on this a little."

His smile was nice. "I could use some help."

"Your courtship will have to be gradual, but you must leave her in no doubt."

"Subtle but positive?" He considered. "I can handle it."

"Convince her, or she'll always think you just settled for what was left. She has a dreadful inferiority complex. God knows how she managed that with us as grandparents, Fred as a father and Phyllis as her mother. None of us ever qualified as a shrinking violet."

"Where is Phyllis now?"

"After she and Harry married, he took her back to Italy. They live in a villa north of Milan. She's doing designs for fabrics, and his current project is adolescents. He is fascinated by the dividing line between childhood and adulthood. His photographs are stunning. We were there last spring. Some of the pictures are so touching. Those young faces with the acceptance of adulthood showing. The arrogance of being alive. The awareness of life. They are thrilling.''

"And Talullah has never forgiven her mother?"

"Talullah blames Phyllis for the entire disaster. Death and desertion are soul shaking for someone as sensitive as Talullah. It's an easy thing to use her mother's desertion as the reason for all heartbreak. She was left alone with just Philo, his sister Agnes, who was very spare and sour, and me. I didn't pay enough attention. It was all such a scandal, and I had always lived a self-centered life of charity committees. I helped everyone else and neglected my own grandchild until it was too late.''

"Don't blame yourself. Everything will work out. Just wait."

"Don't take too long; I'd like to see it."

He leaned down and kissed her cheek...and it was a promise.

After an afternoon of wine tasting Philo Metcalf was just a tad tipsy at dinner and remembered all the pub jokes of his youth. He was hilarious. Talullah laughed until tears came, and watching her, John laughed, too. Mrs. Metcalf smiled with fond patience. She thought jokes were a waste of conversational space.

When John had arrived, it was to see the table already set. Talullah had done it, trying in desperation to fill the time until John came. With nothing left to do, they had gone out to the greenhouse to see Philo and his hoard of homemade wines.

His "cellar" was under the tables that held the plants. The wine bottles rested in stacks of baked clay tubes. Philo had hung burlap from the sides of the tables and thought it was all a delicious secret, but everyone in town knew about Philo's cellar.

No one robbed his cellar. There was small-town honesty, and then there was Killer. Killer was a very large black dog who was suspicious and had an impressive bark and a strong sense of ownership. As long as Philo was around, Killer was like a lamb.

Philo shared his collection lavishly with John, but he allowed Talullah only a sip of each kind. From their trees and vines he had harvested grapes, apples, apricots, pears... Philo used everything. Blackberries, strawberries, whatever. In the corner of the greenhouse, an unruly plant concealed a copper tank with a twisted copper tube.

"Just a sip," Philo warned Talullah. "Nothing worse than a tipsy woman." He belched deliberately for effect and smiled. "Unless it's a tipsy man." He thought that was very funny.

John observed that the straitlaced Talullah was uncharacteristically bland about her grandfather's hobby. How interesting. She was an intricate woman.

At dinner Mildred eventually led them to discuss and contrast towns they'd known and the differences in the people. John was a keen observer of languages, since he was a writer. Philo was observant of habits, Talullah of the children, and Mildred of the organization of services.

After the dishes were loaded into the dishwasher, the food put away and the floor swept, John decided to look at the tennis court before he entered into any further negotiations with Mrs. Metcalf on its restoration.

"You go, Talullah," the old lady instructed in a weakened voice. "I'm just a bit tired."

That was always an out for anyone over eighty. Talullah slid her grandmother a disbelieving look and said ungraciously, "Poor John, he's been gone these eleven years and he's forgotten where the tennis court lies."

John thought how interesting it was that she remembered exactly how long he had been gone.

"Out the front door?" he inquired with an excruciatingly innocent look.

"It's a walk."

"I'm prepared. I've had pigs' knuckles." He held the door for her, and she went out on the big front porch.

"You're really rather strange, John. Is that why you've come back here? Everyone in Tarkington is just a little out of kilter, probably because there's so little new blood. Do you find that here you can seem normal?"

"You've discovered my secret."

"I can't believe the people in Tarkington— however strange they are—can actually compare with anyone on the West Coast."

"People are the same everywhere."

"Frightening, isn't it?"

He would have taken her hand, but she had both hands locked together behind her back. He took seemingly-casual glances at her as they walked through the sprinkling of leaves on the lawn. The trees were magnificent in their fall colors in the setting sun on that perfect day of Indian summer. The air was a better wine than anything Philo had managed.

"I missed the north," John said reflectively. "The fall. The leaves and snow."

"Just wait. You'll miss the California sun and heat."

"I don't think so."

After a dozen or so silent steps, John asked, "Why didn't you marry Pete?"

"I was born to be an old maid." She looked at him, challenging him to try to deny that.

He laughed, a delicious, soft, intimate laugh, and said, "Old maids aren't born; they're made."

Now just what did he mean by that?

## Chapter Two

The Matchmakers of Tarkington were so eager that Mildred Metcalf had some scrambling to do to keep them from ruining everything. "It's because they just don't have enough chances to work at it," she said with a sigh to Sylvia Morrison. Sylvia was her neighbor and grandmother of Paul, who had unknowingly precipitated the whole affair by informing John Peal that Talullah Metcalf was not yet married.

The two old friends were sitting on comfortably padded wicker chairs on the Morrisons' big shaded front porch, with glasses of lemonade and a plate of cookies.

"Don't worry so." Sylvia had another macaroon. "Everything will work out. It's their fate."

"That sounds dreadfully like a firing squad."

"Oh, Mildred, you're so dramatic."

Mildred bent a stern look on her friend and forgave her such a frivolous statement. She had begun some years ago to value the friends who had survived. Mildred was even cordial to Willa Hatterson. Her new tolerance of Willa surprised everyone, but mostly Mildred. After a long enough time even old enemies became precious.

Mrs. Metcalf proclaimed, "I suggest that the best way to handle this is to see to it that they 'just happen' to be together. That way Talullah will become used to John again."

"Mildred, you do remember that they fought like cats and dogs? Or, at least, Talullah did. She is so competitive. And John always teased her so."

"I never noticed."

Remarkably, Sylvia offered no comment as she relished another bite of her cookie. "How do they get along working on the court? Your house is in my way."

"I use my binoculars. My eyes aren't quite as clear as they were, but those army glasses of

Philo's bring them right up as if I could touch them.''

''So?'' Sylvia Morrison encouraged impatiently.

''Well, you know Talullah. She digs in and does more than her share. She works like a mule.''

''When did you ever see a mule work?''

''It's an expression.''

''No hand-holding? Sweaty kisses?''

''You've been reading those romances again.''

John wouldn't work on the court until Talullah was home from school. She complained about that, but he explained, ''I have to write during the day. I make my living writing. Peeling and rolling tennis courts isn't my livelihood, and I'm only being paid in pies and lemonade. I'm surprised Philo allows the fruit to be wasted on anything so silly as pies when it could be put to better use.''

Talullah replied, ''If we took out a section of the wire, we could bring in a tractor.''

''That's the coward's way.''

''You're enjoying this.'' She watched him.

''Very much.''

''You should use a sunscreen,'' she directed. ''You're getting too much sun.'' His body was beautifully tanned, and his muscles were gorgeous. She licked sweat off her upper lip and felt a strange shimmering inside her. She felt very odd when she looked at him. She should wear a hat. It was probably dehydration.

He advised, "Rest awhile. You're not used to this. You could pour me a glass of lemonade."

"I'll sit down, and you can bring me a glass." The Agnes-raised Talullah wasn't one to indulge men. "You've been sitting all day, and the exercise will be good for you. I've been herding a mob of ten-year-olds who would really have preferred to be playing outside."

"I pace when I write," he defended himself.

"Bully."

He leaned his chin on his gloved hands, which rested on the top of the long-handled shovel. "I'll bet that if you'd been born any time in all of history, you would have this same antagonistic competitiveness toward men. For such a feminine woman, your hostility is surprising."

That startled her. "I'm not antimale."

He watched her with deceptively sleepy eyes. "Aren't you?"

"Not at all. I just don't want to have to serve someone because he's male and I happen to be female."

"Men serve women."

"Sexually?"

John smiled. "No. In care and protection."

"I've never had male care and protection."

"Philo."

"He never really noticed I was around."

"He loves you very much."

"Not especially. I'm a commitment. He and Mildred had to take me in, but it was Philo's sister, my Great-Aunt Agnes, who actually took care of me. She didn't love me. She saw to it that I was neat and clean and fed. And she influenced me."

"In what way?" he encouraged.

"Self-reliance, pride, duty, honor, country, that sort of thing."

"No love?"

"It's only a word." She stepped away into the shade and gracefully dropped down on some unpeeled weeds.

He dug the shovel effortlessly into the ground, stood erect, then poured two glasses of lemonade from a jug Mrs. Metcalf had provided, before he joined Talullah. She accepted one with a casual thanks and sipped it.

He sprawled down beside her and was conscious that she shifted away from him. Perhaps he smelled sweaty?

He smelled male. He was very disturbing to her, for some reason. And if she weren't quite so close she could look at him more easily.

He was so big. His stomach was hard and flat, and there was a maddening mat of soft curling hair on his chest that the breeze ruffled so carelessly, when her fingers were curious to do exactly that. To distract herself she said, "Tell me about your time away from Tarkington."

"It was very interesting. People are basically the same everywhere. For every Philo there's a Bert Hooker. For every Mildred Metcalf there's a Sylvia Morrison. For every Talullah Metcalf, there's a Cindy Bates."

"Cindy?" She frowned at John. "How do Cindy and I contrast?"

"You don't know?"

"She's blond and I'm brunette?"

"She's very open."

"You consider me closed-up?"

He chose his words carefully. "How about private."

"In what way?"

"You hide."

"I'm just like everyone else." But her voice was a little strident, and her words sounded defensive.

"Don't be afraid of me, Talullah."

"I'm not. I learned not to trust you when I was six."

"Six?" He was indignant.

"Before that it was open to debate; after six I never trusted you again."

"What did I do?" he demanded.

"Whatever you could to annoy or horrify or tease me."

"I need a good PR man."

"No need." She was indifferent. "I've learned not to be so trusting."

He was appalled.

Things didn't go very well. Talullah concentrated on her kids at school. The tennis court was finished, and the Metcalfs had to post a reserve schedule. As it always happens, if someone else will fix the court, there's no end to those who will use it. John and Talullah did play. He was superb; she was out of practice, but she didn't give up or allow him to be easy with her.

Then the weather changed. October relinquished its place to November. The winds blew cold; the leaves fell in drifts, and there was the first dusting of snow. It was time for Talullah's grandparents to make their yearly retreat to Florida.

"I'll drive them to Indy to the airport," John told Talullah one day as Mildred checked lists.

"No need," Talullah replied. "I always do it."

"We could take them down and go to Keystone at the Crossing and have dinner," John offered.

"If you insist on driving, it *would* be easier for me. I need the time to plan for the Christmas play."

"I thought we could go together."

"No need for both of us. I'll take them down."

"Talullah, you're being difficult."

She looked at him, puzzled. "I am? I *said* I'd take them. You aren't involved! How could I be the one who's being difficult? You started this whole thing by offering to take them to the airport; now I'm being difficult. You don't make any sense at all."

She was too used to avoiding any involvement. But John was discouraged. He'd been there two months, and he was no further along with her than when he'd arrived. She simply didn't understand that she was being courted.

He told Mrs. Metcalf, "I ought to just tell her that I want to marry her."

"I can't think of anything that would put her

off more. Then she would know what you intend and be more on guard than ever and avoid any contact. You must be patient. It could take a year!''

''I don't want to wait a year.''

''Men.''

''I get to take you to the airport.'' He waited pointedly. ''Alone.''

''At least you didn't both refuse. I'd dislike hitchhiking in this weather.'' Mrs. Metcalf rather liked dramatic imagery.

''The only reason I want to marry Talullah is to get you in my family.''

''I know, darling, and it's worth all the effort. I suppose you realize I've made Talullah my sole heir?''

''You didn't have a lot of choice,'' he said needlessly.

''I could have left everything to Prissy.''

''I've never seen a more peculiar cat.''

''It comes from being alone.'' Mrs. Metcalf paused deliberately before she added, ''Like Talullah.''

''Talullah is knee-deep in grandparents.''

''For all the good it does her. She has never learned to love. Not even her cat. She cares for it. That's all.''

"What do I do?"

"Be with her. Be gentle. Be patient."

"I think I'll become a monk." John liked dramatic imagery, too.

"It would be too serene. You would be bored."

"I find I'm very sad and lonely."

"Want to visit us down in Florida? You can write there, too. And your grandparents would drive you mad showing you off."

"I guess that means it would be better if I stayed here and worked on Talullah."

"Everyone in town is rooting for you. And you'll be astonished at how cleverly you will constantly see each other."

"The Matchmakers." He sighed.

"Let them help you."

"Why can't we just arrange this marriage between us and make Talullah submit? Once she's married to me, she won't mind it."

"Sex is the answer?"

"It would help me."

"But, John, you want her love. You'll have to teach her to realize she loves you and needs you."

"How in the hell can I do that?"

"You're a brilliant man. You're imaginative and insightful. You will win."

"Thanks, Coach."

All during that time, everything that happened in Tarkington, every single occasion, meeting, or discussion, required the presence of two particular people: John and Talullah.

As was her way, Talullah was unstinting in her participation. She gave time, thought and energy whenever she was asked. Finally she was stretched almost too far. John had to ask the Matchmakers to back off a little, to choose their meetings a little less wildly. They were exhausting Talullah.

And he could see no indication that she felt any differently about him than she ever had.

It was about then that Talullah began to dream of a phantom lover.

Strange, she'd never dreamed of men. She hadn't been particularly conscious of even dreaming. She worked hard, and she went to bed tired. She slept. But now she began to dream.

He would come to her, this phantom lover. He would smile, but strain as she would, she couldn't distinguish his features. He would take off his clothes and sit on her bed, and then she would watch as he turned toward her.

Since it was very obvious that he wasn't there to play Tiddlywinks, the sleeping Talullah was always shocked to such an extent that her conscience wakened her. How irritating. She got to the point that she would resist waking. But then he would rise and walk away from her, or a danger of some kind would interfere, or something would happen to prevent him from leaning over, so beautifully naked, and begin kissing her.

It was maddening. In all her life Talullah had never seen a grown man naked. Babies, little kids, but never a grown man. She was so curious.

It was difficult to look at men on the beach or at the pool or down at Tarkington's water hole by the river. There was no subtle way to stare. When a woman stared at a man, the man thought it was a come-on. She wasn't being inviting; she was only curious. Their bodies were so marvelously made. The intricate and varied patterns of hair, the long sinuous muscles, the shape and power of the muscles moving under their smooth skins. Beautiful.

The most attractive men were those who seemed unaware of themselves, who moved and walked without trying to garner attention. It wasn't the exhibitionists who lured her eyes, but the men who were so comfortable with their bodies that they ignored them. Those who sought to be admired didn't seem quite as masculine as those who simply accepted the fact that they were male.

They tempted her to stare. And so did John. She could close her eyes and remember his tanned, muscled body as he worked on the tennis court, and she would be filled with a strange restlessness. She would pace the house and scrub the kitchen floor. She would toss in her spinster bed and tangle up the sheets and blankets. Prissy would become quite irritated with her.

She had never been this way. It had been years since she'd accepted the fact that she would never marry. Why now? Why this disturbance? This restlessness that had nothing to do with idleness? She wasn't idle. There weren't enough hours in the day for all the demands on her time, and yet she was discontented, impatient, and prey to a longing she didn't understand.

It wasn't school. That was satisfying. The kids had settled in, and she was pleased to see the variety that made a good class. The shooting stars tugged the laggards along and stimulated the plodding middle-of-the-roaders. She never admitted to having pets. All of them were precious. But this year there was Bobby Parker, who gladdened her heart. He was such a sparkling-eyed rascal. He had such humor. Some of it was killing. He would fall into routines just to get a laugh. He needed to be more secure in himself.

He could do that by studying. Right now he used humor and teasing to be liked. If he could put as much work into his studies, he wouldn't need to be such a disruptive clown. Talullah was working on that, though he wasn't terribly interested. His grammar was atrocious, but how could she teach a kid to speak well when his parents cheerfully destroyed any sentence? When there were teachers whose grammar was as bad as his? How could anybody go through college and still speak poorly?

And then there was Benjamin Ketrick. He was living in Tarkington now, with his Uncle Bill and Aunt Sue. His father had died in Central America eight years ago, when Benjamin was only two, and last summer his mother died, too. Benjamin was a troubled child. How long did grief take to pass?

Feeling the need to talk to someone, Talullah called Linda out in Seattle. It turned out to be a fruitless conversation; when she asked the routine "How's it going?" Linda replied, "Chicken pox." The two words said it all.

"That doesn't happen in the fall; it happens in the spring!"

"I'll tell the kids," Linda promised immediately, then added, "I'm going crazy."

Heartlessly Talullah reminded her, "You said you would take Mark over friendship."

"Every time." Linda's reply was immediate, and it was nice to hear her say that. Then Linda said, "There's really nothing to keep you there in Tarkington; why don't you come out to the great, beautiful state of Washington, specifically to Seattle? I'd even help you find an apartment."

"This is my home, my native land." That was what John had said, she realized.

"At least I chose a real live human being as my life's commitment. You chose a town like Tarkington."

"It's special."

"Yes," Linda readily agreed.

"You admit that out loud?"

"I get lonesome for Tarkington."

"Me, too. When we were away at college, I knew we'd both be coming home again."

There was a little silence, then Linda said, "Mark's worth it."

"Even with the kids' chicken pox?"

"Definitely. Without Mark there wouldn't be any chicken pox."

"I've never heard anything so romantic in my life." Talullah laughed.

"It is, isn't it? I'll make him a coconut cream pie for supper tonight, and it'll knock him right off his feet, he'll feel so special."

"Insidious tactics."

"And fun."

The conversation didn't help Talullah; it just made her more restless.

Another restless resident of Tarkington was John Peal. He spent a lot of time staring out over the countryside from his house on the other side of town from Talullah as he tried to think how to attract her.

He got up from his desk and his ignored Apple II Plus, to walk into his bedroom and look dispiritedly into his mirror.

He was tall enough; he weighed enough and not too much. His body was okay. He stared at his face. Zero. He rubbed his chin. Maybe after Christmas he'd grow whiskers. If she didn't like them, he could shave them off; if she did, bingo.

He considered Talullah. She was like no woman he'd ever known. She was so sleek, so graceful, and his body craved her. So did his eyes. His mind. She was perfect.

How could he convince her that she ought to marry him and give him exclusive rights to her life and love? How mind-boggling that she was still unmarried. How had that happened? How could he have been so lucky as to have this opportunity to court and win her?

Court and win. He was doing a lousy job of it. Mildred Metcalf had called him yesterday for a progress report. No progress. John sighed, put on his jogging suit and went out to run. Maybe if his blood was moving his brain would work.

He ran easily, clearing his mind so it would be receptive to ideas. He programmed it to approach this problem, inventively. It worked with plots. This situation was exactly that—a plot. That it wasn't fiction made no difference.

Yes, it did. The difference was that in fiction the writer could work both sides. He could contrive the reaction to make the plot work. But in real life he could run his butt off and still not get Talullah to react the way he wanted her to.

He wanted her to look at him with awareness. He wanted her pupils to dilate and her lips to part and her breath to pause. He wanted her to come to him and put her hands on him, lift her mouth to his and whisper his name.

As he ran he put his hand to his forehead to

clear his mind, but the vision stayed. He could feel her breath against his mouth, and then her lips.... Her body touched his as she leaned against him....

Brakes squealed, and John jerked to a stop. He lifted both hands out in apology.

"Bet you're over your head in plots for your books, right?" It was Jim Uler. "You ought to pay attention to the real world. I guess the rest of us have to look out for you geniuses and see you don't get run over!" He lifted a hand and drove away.

Jim had thought that he was concentrating on writing when he could only think of seducing Tal-ullah Metcalf, and indifferent spinster school-teacher. How could anyone ever see Talullah as a spinster, for God's sake?

If he could ever get her free of the wall that imprisoned her soul, they would all see her as he did, as the warm, loving, tender-hearted woman of any man's dream.

He had to be careful that no other man saw her that way until he was safely married to her. He couldn't risk having a more attractive man cap-turing her away from him. She was his. She'd been his all her life. How was it that she didn't know it? It was so obvious to him. They were meant for each other. He'd always known.

He would never forget the poleaxed feeling that had come over him when he heard she was engaged to Pete. That he'd lost her! How had it happened? All hope vanished. He was sunk. She was to marry Pete. No man that close to possessing her would ever give her up.

John had been in despair. He'd turned to his writing and poured his soul into it. His anguish. His dreams. How amazing that his books had sold. Think of all the anguished people who had responded to his writing. Was all the world peopled with those who had lost in love?

Then Paul Morrison had brought the stunning news that she had never married!

He could not allow himself to flub this miraculous second chance. He had to win her this time, any way he could. If he could just get her to marry him, her sense of commitment would keep her with him, and eventually he could teach her to love him. Couldn't he? How was he to accomplish this task?

After all those days of plots and plans, he thought her grandmother was probably right. Tallullah needed space. She needed to grow accustomed to the idea of him before he could begin to actually court her. He would pretend that women and marriage were the last things on his mind. He would treat her like a friend. He would treat her as if he weren't interested in romance. Could he do that? Well, he could try.

He'd take her fishing. That's what he'd do. He'd treat her as if she were just another guy. Ordinary. As if he didn't crave her. As if he didn't want to hold her head in his hands as he kissed her mindless. As if his hands didn't want to caress and explore and soothe her body.

How could he? If it worked, it would be worth the effort.

He shook his head as he jogged and groused aloud, "Talullah, you are such a pain." She was. Sweet pain. Mind-bending pain. Exquisite pain. Damn.

How would he survive?

They went fishing. He borrowed a boat, and they went out on the White River. They dressed warmly, because it was a gloomy day with a biting wind. The water was warmer than the air, and the fish were not indifferent.

She caught the most fish. He wasn't paying any attention, and as usual, she totally concentrated on the job at hand. She was fishing, ergo she caught fish.

She was businesslike and dedicated, and she ignored the fact that he was a man. It was disconcerting. Other women found him exciting. He'd had women *pursue* him! Why couldn't Talullah?

It made him short-tempered, and she ignored that, too. She allowed him to set out their lunch, even accepted that he should. That galled him. Women had stumbled over their feet to serve him and please him. Why couldn't Talullah want to please him?

In his mind, as he lay back in the boat, snugly dressed in waterproof clothing to suit the lousy weather, he thought of Talullah serving him. No wonder he didn't catch any fish. Talullah took his pole out of his indifferent hands and brought in a beauty, which she thoughtlessly put into her own creel.

It was a good thing she didn't know her fate. She wouldn't be so relaxed and smug. She'd get wary and careful. He, too, could be careful. He was going to win. Her.

## Chapter Three

The first time Talullah talked to John about the Matchmakers was when they were on the committee in charge of decorating the Presbyterian church for the school Christmas play, which was to be held early in December. The church had the largest seating capacity in Tarkington, and it was more Christmassy than the school gym.

Talullah and John were alone in the church when she said to him, "Well, brace yourself. They have decided we should get married." She handed him the end of a garland as he teetered his big, gorgeous male body on an unreliable ladder.

"Who has?" He froze at her words. She knew! But outwardly he appeared to be paying more attention to the placement of the garland than to her reply.

"The town matchmakers. That includes just about anyone and either sex."

"You ought not to say that word in church!" His blue eyes glinted humorously as he looked down at Talullah's brown ones.

"What word? Matchmaker?"

Back to draping the garland, he replied, "Sex."

"Doesn't God know about sex? Of course he does. He made Eve for Adam."

"Odd wordage for an eighties' woman."

She squinted. "Sex is an odd word?"

"No. Admitting God made Eve *for* Adam. It's a revealing thing to say. Women are made for men."

"No, no, no. God made men first so they could clear things away; then women could arrive to find everything tidy. Unfortunately, God had no idea that if anyone else is available, men naturally delegate things. After Eve arrived, men rested on their laurels and expected women to take over and do everything else."

"See?" he proclaimed righteously. "We intended to share the load all along."

"...under men's supervision," she corrected.

"You women have to learn to do things right. Therefore you must be supervised." He reached out to loop the garland over the next hook, and the rickety ladder wobbled.

She flung out a useless hand and warned, "Be careful."

"It appears to me that I am working under *your* supervision." His deep voice was droll as he gave her a brief, lofty look.

"I didn't want to risk climbing the ladder."

"But you're perfectly willing to risk me." He was indignant.

"You heal fast. I assured myself of that. I remember your football years and Mary Beth hovering over your battered body."

"Ah, Mary Beth," he said in a reminiscent manner. "Five kids and pregnant again."

"Naturally."

"She was always impulsive."

"What's that supposed to mean?"

He chuckled, his eyes dancing, but he didn't reply.

Huffily Talullah continued, "By purest accident I overheard us being discussed. The reason we're on this committee is that they have made the decision. That's why we did the Halloween party and the senior class bus trip. They are in earnest. They are deliberately throwing us together.''

He intoned, ''We control our own destinies.'' Apparently she didn't yet suspect the extent of the Matchmakers' conspiracy.

''You have ostrich blood,'' she declared hotly.

''Where?''

''In your sand-buried head. You have to pay attention, or we'll end up married.''

''There is no way I'm getting married,'' he ventured cautiously, sticking to his plan of indifference. ''I still have years left for being a carefree rake. I shouldn't be denied my opportunity. I'm not ready to settle down and be a husband and father. But when that time comes, I'll choose my own wife.''

''Who?''

''I don't know yet. When I start looking,'' he said, looking down at her, ''I'll recognize her immediately.''

''Look around and you'll see that there aren't that many young women for you to choose from. You'll have to go down several age brackets and raid the seniors in high school.''

''Really? I like them young. Get 'em young

and raise 'em right. Good motto. I'll get the pick of the crop.''

''You have a careless attitude,'' Talullah informed him critically. ''My grandfather always said a man picks a woman like an apple picks a farmer.''

He climbed down the ladder, then shifted it to another place. As he climbed back up he said, ''Quit worrying. You have no reason to be afraid of me.''

''Have you noticed that no one has come into the church? They're all busy other places in order to leave us alone so we'll look into each other's eyes and realize we're made for each other.''

He laughed immoderately.

Talullah sighed. ''John, you have to take this seriously. Our lives are in danger.''

''You were always dramatic.''

''I have never been dramatic! I am sober and in control. But *I* recognize hazards. This is one. I will be thirty in two months, and you are thirty-one. They think—''

''My God, you're going to be *thirty?*'' He stopped what he was doing and looked down at her in surprise.

''Thirty comes quite naturally after twenty-nine," she retorted. "I am now twenty-nine, and on my next birthday I shall be thirty."

"You're an old maid," he observed cheerfully. He was again looking at the garland and missed her slight flinch.

"It's called career woman now. 'Old maid' dates you."

"What old maid dates me?"

"Good grief, John, will you quit being frivolous? This is serious! Are you completely unaware? Are you so dense you don't recognize the danger? I believe you played too many football games without your helmet."

"You're cluttered with obsolete sayings. That one was funny fifteen years ago."

"I was making a point."

"Be more original."

"All right. In words of one syllable: look out! You could soon be…uh…wed to me."

"I appreciate your warning, but there's no problem. I'm an unconsenting adult. Don't give it another thought."

"You were away from Tarkington for how long?"

"The last time? It was about—what? Four years? No. Five? It must be over eight years."

"It's been eleven."

"I came back eight years ago. You weren't here. You were engaged to Pete." He glanced down at her.

"You don't remember much, do you?"

He smiled that smile of his that could make a woman think he found her excessively attractive. "I remember quite a bit. Nothing's changed."

"People always say that nothing's changed. They look around and smile and are glad. But then they leave again, because that's why they left in the first place. Nothing ever changes here."

"Would you want it to?"

"I hate seeing our brightest leaving. I hate supplying the rest of the world with our best."

"I came back."

"For how long? Until you decide to settle down? Then you'll go out into the world to seek a bride. Or will you bring one home, where she'll have to try for her entire lifetime to fit in and catch up on all the history of the place? She would be an outsider all her life. And there's no one else for you here but me. They have decided that we should marry."

"It's only your imagination. You've always been imaginative. Remember the wolfman?"

"He used to give me nightmares."

"Why would that bother you? All across the

Midwest there are periodic outbreaks of sightings. Nothing ever comes of it. It's a tradition, like the Matchmakers. Nowadays no one has the time to be a wolfman…or a matchmaker.''

"John, small towns are *notorious* for this, and Tarkington's the worst. There's only one movie theater, and there's nothing else for people to *do!*''

"You let it bother you. Why? All you have to do is be determined to run your own life. Like I am. Nobody tells me what to do. I do things my way.''

He came down the ladder and smiled that unfair smile at her as he gave her a brotherly pat on the shoulder. She looked at him and gave an exasperated sigh. "I don't want to marry you.''

He paused to tell her reasonably, "I haven't asked you.''

"Thank you.''

He moved the ladder again. "I always liked your mother.''

"Did you?''

"Do you miss her?''

"It's been a long time.''

Surveying their work, he commented, "Our grandparents are good friends.''

"Yes.''

"Do you ever feel alone here—with them off wintering in Florida?"

"How could I?"

"Well, you didn't have any brothers or sisters."

With some impatience Talullah replied, "If I had, they would probably have moved away, too."

"I think your mother is happy where she is."

"She's weird. Dad said so."

He adjusted the shaky ladder. "Your father was prosaic."

"I take after him."

John burst into laughter, and she waited with great patience for him to control it.

"The only interesting thing about your father, Talullah, was his getting hit by a train. Anyone would have bet good money he'd die quietly in bed of a nice dignified everyday, run-of-the-mill disease."

"You're rude."

"Considering how long I've known you, I think I'm allowed a touch of rudeness here and there." He rudely ruffled her hair as he would a child's. Sentimentally he remembered, "We've known each other all our lives. In Sunday school you wore the same dress every week, and your braids were so tight your eyes slanted.''

"It wasn't the same dress. I had several; but they were always brown. I hated the color until my mother said, 'It makes your eyes so beautiful.' I still feel pretty when I wear brown.''

He gave her a quick look. He'd never realized that she had ever wanted to look pretty. It anguished him so much that he couldn't think of anything to say. She too, was silent. Finally, to break the silence, he asked, "Uh…how's Bobby doing?''

Bobby was the problem child in her fourth-grade class. "He'll shrug his shoulders and say, 'Beats me,' because he saw it on TV and people laughed. He tried it in class, and the other kids laughed, so he does it endlessly. He's driving me mad! But it's Ben I worry about.''

"Why?'' He gave her a quick look because her voice was so serious. Troubled.

"He's not recovering from his grief. He's too quiet.''

"I thought that's what you worked for: quiet, obedient kids.''

"Not that dull eyed and quiet.''

He worked at the garland and was silent.

She asked, "Why did you really come back to Tarkington?"

"Ohhh…" He began a quick search for reasons besides her. "I was lonely. I was a stranger in L.A. I missed people waving and calling greetings on the street. I missed everyone knowing my business and remembering what my dad and mother had done. I missed the grandparents. I missed having the old gossips telling each other things and tracing back my traits through my forebears and knowing I was a part of a continuing line. And I'm doing the research and writing down all that stuff and making a book about it."

She responded knowingly, "To make a greater fortune so you can leave again."

He took up the thread. "And live with Philo in the south of France and watch the vineyards grow more wine for our consumption."

"It's just as well. You go ahead. We don't need any more lazy citizens here; we need some vibrant, active ones. You write your book and leave." She flipped her hand as if she was flicking off a fly. Then she tilted her head thoughtfully as she added, "I'm glad you dismiss the Matchmakers. I'm glad to hear of your ambitions—such as they are. I'm glad I'm safe from you. For I am. You're the last man in this town for me, but I wouldn't marry you if you were the last man on earth." She said it blithely, as if she had been freed from some obligation. Or temptation?

He was blank faced in astonishment, but she smiled as she reached up rudely and patted his cheek—as one would a child's—then she walked over to the storage box and pulled out the next garland. "Here you go," she said cheerily. "Only two more."

He frowned at her thoughtfully, then tested the ladder as his eyes measured the remaining hooks. He climbed up before he reached down to grasp the end of the garland. Although she commented now and then, his replies had become monosyllabic. She appeared not to notice.

After a time she asked, "When did you start smoking?"

"I don't."

"But you did. I suspect Bobby's smoking."

"It won't kill him."

"Oh?"

"Well, he's young."

"When did you start?"

"I must have been twelve. My dad gave me a cigar, but I wasn't dumb. I knew my mother would have a fit, so I took it out in back of the garage, lit up and was very careful not to inhale.

Dad came looking for me about half an hour later, and I smiled at him clear-eyed and pink cheeked and healthy. He didn't know what to say."

"You always did figure the angles. I'm surprised you're not a gambler in Las Vegas."

"You are casting mud at a fine upstanding man whose lofty gaze..."

"...comes from standing on a very shaky ladder." She laughed.

"Oh, that's it! I thought I was levitating."

"Shame on you!"

"God has to have the best sense of humor in all of His creation."

Quite sassily she replied, "You're living proof."

"So you admit I'm one of God's creatures and not the spawn of the devil?"

"The jury is still out."

He complained, "I've had trouble with your having a conscience ever since the watermelon caper all those years ago. As I said at the time, Talullah, there are circumstances when it's imperative not to tell the truth."

"When one tells the truth, St. Peter erases a black mark on your book of sins."

"You must have piled up, unused, a stack of

erasures just…'' But his tongue stopped as he saw that her cheeks were pink. "Why, Talullah! You're blushing!'' That brought him down from the ladder in a bound, and he caught her as she turned away, slapping at his hands. But he wasn't put off. "Oh, no, you don't! This is incredible! Talullah, what *have* you done? What lascivious thoughts have blotched up your heavenly copybook? Confess, and I'll put in a good word for you.''

That was such a ridiculous thought that she sputtered with laughter as she ducked her head, trying to hide her face from him.

So, of course, Mrs. Peterson walked in on the pair right then, with Talullah struggling in John's arms, and John coaxing while Talullah protested and blushed. It thrilled Mrs. Peterson to her toenails to actually witness raw passion in the flesh that way, and she was the hissing, whispering marvel of the week. "Well, my dear, you cannot believe…'' But everyone did—avidly.

So the next day, when Talullah met John in the snow in front of Mr. Hooker's drugstore, she started out without even a greeting. "Mrs. Peterson caught us in a passionate embrace inside the *church*, and everyone is tittering over it.''

"Embrace?" He tried to remember anything even similar that could have been misconstrued.

"When you jumped off the ladder and tried to wrestle me around."

He laughed. "I was trying to see that blush from your sinful, guilty conscience. What's lying there, rotting on your soul? Have you murdered someone? Said something catty? What sin's bothering you so much you have to blush? Do you have a telescope and you're watching the boys at gym?"

"I can't understand why you aren't seeing this information in the context of our problem."

"Honey, if you have a problem, tell your uncle John about it. I have all sorts of means to soothe the troubled female breast. Let's just step into my car, and I'll take you home with me, to my office there, and you can bare your…soul."

"It's just this sort of levity that could entrap us in an impossible situation, John. You *must* understand!"

Perhaps it was the crisp day with its new covering of fresh snow. Perhaps he was feeling unusually well. Perhaps his book was going nicely. God only knows why he did it, but he laughed at her fears, reached out and took her knitted cap from her head, tumbling her hair down around her shoulders. Then he backed up two steps and held her cap just out of her reach.

She was furious with him. He was being obtuse, teasing her, acting just the way she'd longed for him to act toward her—fourteen years ago. But time and maturity had cured her obsession with him. That and the mirror. Reality.

She glared at him and he laughed. She knew exactly the threat he represented to other women. She stomped her foot then looked down in shock that her foot had done something so adolescent. She stupidly grabbed for the cap, and of course, he simply lifted it out of her reach.

How childish! But frustration was boiling in her, and she reached down, scooped up a handful of snow—and threw it at him! Her mind watched the whole stupid charade, simply appalled.

Abandoning her hat, she flipped around and stormed off. He chased after her, pulled the hat down over her head, all the way over her face to her chin, blinding her. Then the idiot held her hands, preventing her from tearing it off. She tried to kick his shins, and he laughed the entire time.

How humiliating. Such conduct!

The town loved it. Talullah seriously considered moving to Indianapolis and anonymity.

\*   \*   \*

With her grandparents in Florida for the winter, Talullah was alone. She lived in the Metcalf home as naturally as she breathed, nestled between other big houses and nosy neighbors who watched out for her. And then there was Prissy, her cat, who was an autocrat. Philo's moonshine was safely locked in the basement, under controlled temperatures for the winter, Killer having gone to Florida with the Metcalfs. He was having a rest from guarding Philo's wines.

Talullah's bed was a four-poster with a canopy of lace that had been hand-crocheted by her great-grandmother. Talullah had mended it and rehung it two years before, and when she washed it in the summers, she did it outside on the lawn in a series of tubs, lifting it gently and being very careful when she laid it out on the grass to bleach and dry.

It was in that bed that she now dreamed. As stiff and spare as she was in real life, in her dreams she had become lush and desirable. She knew with some cynicism that it had to be a dream, because no man alive had ever affected her as did the phantom in her thoughts.

She wished there was someone with whom she could discuss the dreams, to find out why she had them. She knew it couldn't possibly be frustration at being alone, because she was alone by choice.

So why the dreams? Was it old Mother Nature? Was it the instinct for mating and having children that God had put into us all like embedded computer commands in order to continue the race? Did other women experience such dreams? Why had they come now? Who could she ask? Who could she ask who wouldn't gossip about her questions?

It was irritating to dream that way. She spent many nights trying to get the phantom to show his face. He never did—until one night...

That night the phantom sat naked on her bedside. His gorgeous body was shadowed by the lace canopy, and the dusky hair that furred him curled, inviting her fingers. His muscles bunched as he turned to her. Her eyes strained anxiously, and she saw his face.

The phantom was John Peal.

## Chapter Four

John Peal? Her phantom lover? How ridiculous! It showed how foolish dreams are. It was as if he had deliberately invaded her dream just to annoy her. If he would know about the dreams, he would do that, thinking it was very, very funny. And he would laugh.

He would laugh exactly the way he'd laughed long ago after he held out his closed hand and said he had a present for her. She'd foolishly trusted him and reached for it. When she'd shrieked over the tiny snake, he'd laughed. Then, when she'd cried, he'd been annoyed and called her a baby.

However, just after that, Syd Roper had thrown a spider on her, and John had pushed him over. That was an odd thing to remember. John had probably pushed Syd over because he was the only one who was allowed to torment "Talullah Baby." That was what he'd called her from then clear through high school, until his family had moved to New York State.

John was an irritating man. She had made it very clear just what she thought of him. And in those years, she'd cried buckets of tears.

She slept again and was restless until her dream returned. It was summer this time. She was in her dream bed—which looked exactly like her own—and the summer night's breeze lifted the lace window curtains. Her lips parted and she smiled faintly...expectantly.

He came through the window, naked as always, his body screened by the lace curtain. She strained to see him, but by then he was sitting on her bed. Soon he would turn to her. She breathed shallowly, waiting. He turned slowly, his muscled body beautiful, and—it was John Peal again!

Even in her dream she was mad. She stood up on the bed and furiously slung a pillow at him, and, predictably, he laughed. He stood up, unabashedly naked, his feet apart, his hands on his hips, and he laughed. All he needed to finish it off was to call her Talullah Baby.

Then the faint amused sound echoed in her ears as the dream fragmented, and his deep whisper said, "Talullah Baby."

She awakened again, fully and sourly. How like him to disturb the one beautiful thing in her life. Having the phantom call her that hated name proved it was her own censoring mind that intruded in her wicked erotic fantasies.

Why did she think they were wicked dreams? Who did they harm? It was such an innocent thing. She never, well, the phantom never... She always awakened in time.

Irritating her cat, she turned over and looked out her window at the still dark winter morning. The snow was beautiful on the house tops. The Millers needed more insulation. The heat escaping from the attic had melted the snow on their roof. Their chimney was ringed with birds toasting their bottoms on the hot air rising from the furnace.

A cardinal flew into the bare branches by her window and sat sassily. Sparrows quickly surrounded him, chirping at him. He was annoyed and jumped at one, who only hopped to another branch just out of reach. None of the others even moved as they continued to chirp.

The cardinal jumped at several more, and the same thing happened each time. What nastiness were the smaller birds saying to the cardinal to make him so angry? It sounded so fresh and cheerful to her, but it was making the red bird mad. Were the sparrows taunting him? Daring him?

It was a good lesson in unity. The sparrows were much smaller, but, joined together, they could defeat the larger bird.

Who could she get to help her gang up on John? The problem was that if he jumped toward any other woman, she wouldn't jump away. *That was it!* She'd find another woman for the Matchmakers to throw at John! They'd marry him off, she'd be free of matchmaking, and she could have her dream phantom back again.

Who? What woman? She shook the town's population in her mental hopper to get rid of those who were committed, and she came up with Cindy Bates, who wasn't exactly engaged.

As Talullah rose, showered and dressed, she considered her candidate. Cindy was twenty-six and the owner of the best and most expensive beauty salon in Tarkington. It was housed in a separate building instead of being in the basement of her home. There were even potted palms set artfully around, and she had an exhaust system so the smell of the permanents, hair spray and goop didn't ruin customers' lungs.

Talullah had just finished her breakfast that morning when her doorbell rang. It was early for anyone to be up—unless John Peal was ruining their favorite dreams, too. Who should she find on her doorstep, stomping snow off her boots, but Cindy Bates! How providential!

"I was just thinking of you." Talullah greeted the younger woman with unusual good cheer as she invited her inside.

"Talullah," Cindy began stridently, "I've come to do something about your hair. The Christmas fairy can't look like an MTV reject. I'm only going to shape it. It will grow, and you can whack it off again whenever you choose, in your own inimitable way, but for the play I'm going to have it shaped. No argument. It's my Christmas gift to the town."

Talullah smiled and said, "Fine. How nice of you. I'll pay, of course. You're sweet to come here to do it. A house call?"

"Yeah." Cindy's jaw went slack at Talullah's

ready capitulation before she narrowed her eyes and frowned suspiciously. "What's up?"

"Not a thing." Talullah smiled benignly as she led Cindy to her kitchen. "You even brought a cape?" She was friendly. "You *are* prepared. How about the stool?" She dragged it over into the middle of the kitchen floor and sat on it docilely.

"Okay." Cindy put her tools on a newspaper on the counter and flipped the plastic cape over Talullah before she put a white paper collar under the neck of the cape and fastened it. "I've been wanting to get my hands on your hair for years, Talullah."

"Don't frighten me."

"I swear I'll only shape it. You would look fantastic with it shorter, but I'll only shape it."

Talullah raised inquiring brows as she asked, "You do know I have to be at school by 7:45?"

"Be quiet."

"Is that a good attitude toward a 'faithful customer' like me?" Talullah hadn't been inside a beauty salon in a good ten years.

"I can't chat. I have to plan."

"You mean this is a science?" Talullah was enjoying herself.

"I may snip off your ear."

"How would you cut John Peal's hair?"

"Who would care?"

Talullah smiled. "He needs a wife."

"I thought the town had decided on you."

"But John and I disagree. John and I are zilch. No attraction at all. Zero. He's about as exciting as a plain brother."

Cindy muttered, "I'd like a try at him."

"Be my guest."

"You're sure?" Even her scissors paused.

"Positive."

Again the scissors snipped busily away. After a time Cindy said, "I dream about him."

"Oh? Do you?" There *were* others! "What do you dream?" Talullah held her breath.

"I dream he comes into my bedroom and takes off his clothes and gets in bed with me. It started the day in September, when he came back to town and went down to the river, took off his shirt and swam in his shorts. My God."

"Really?" Talullah did a credible job of being casual and not too curious. "And he makes love to you?"

"Something always interrupts. I don't think he really wants to. I have the feeling he discovers he's in the wrong bed and is nice about it, but he never does anything."

"John was always irritating as a child."

"I wonder if he'd marry me. I'd hate to give up Pat if John wasn't interested."

"Pat's a nice guy," Talullah stated firmly.

"He was very helpful after Charles took off and left me with the salon just started and needing so much done. I don't know what I would have done without Pat."

"You like him?"

"Yeah." Cindy was silent. "But I would like a shot at John."

"Why not?"

"If I could I'd spray fixative on Pat and hold him in suspension until I decided on whether or not I wanted John."

"Every woman should have a choice." Talullah was emphatic.

"I think I'll try him. You're sure you're not interested?"

"Not at all."

"You're a born old maid." Cindy wasn't being critical. It was a widely accepted observation.

"Yeah. And can you imagine the townspeople trying to be matchmakers for me?"

"It's your attitude," Cindy explained. "You'd be nice enough looking if you'd give yourself a chance. You need a little makeup. You ought to take better care of your skin. Men like soft skin. You ought to use sunscreen. You'll get blotchy.''

''That sounds attractive.''

''You're careless with yourself,'' Cindy said as if stating the obvious.

''You mean I take off my glasses and let down my hair and poof! I'm a beauty?'' Talullah flung out her hand under the cape, dislodging a cascade of clipped hair.

''You're not bad.'' Cindy stepped away and squinted at her victim. She moved around her, combing a lot and taking a careful snip here or there. ''Okay. Now go look.'' She undid the cape carefully and folded it up to keep the rest of the clipped hair trapped.

Talullah put her hands up, ran her fingers through the mass and smiled uncertainly. ''It feels different.''

Cindy was watching her with a strange expression. ''You look different.''

And she did.

Talullah was briefly shocked but covered it with a courteous smile at Cindy, who refused payment, ''No. As I said, it's my gift to the town to make the Christmas Fairy look good. You look great. Even better than I thought you would. You need to keep your hair nice.''

"It's clean." By then the tidy Talullah was sweeping up the rest of the clippings.

"So's your kitchen floor," Cindy grated, making Talullah grin as Cindy collected her things before she marched to the front door. "Thanks for the try at John. You are sure? He might get interested when he sees your hair that way."

"I wouldn't want a man who only saw the surface."

"Hah!" Cindy put on her boots, stuffed her arms into her coat sleeves and gave a half-wave as she left.

Talullah waited, disciplining herself, then slowly went to the big mirror over the sideboard in the dining room.

It was she. That lovely sleek woman staring blankly back at her from the mirror was she. Somehow the plain features of her ordinary face were enhanced by the shining flow of her shaped hair. How amazing. It was a while before she could tear her eyes away from her image to gather her school things and put on her coat and boots. It was late, so she couldn't walk; she had to drive her car.

By the time she got to school, she had scoffed herself into realizing that it must have been the shadows in the dining room and the orderly hair that had given her the illusion that she looked different.

But the kids exclaimed, "Hey, Ms. Metcalf, you look nice!" That was the word they used: nice. Except Bobby. He said she was beautiful. The other kids hooted and laughed at him, so he shrugged his shoulders and said, "Beats me." And things got back to normal.

The principal, Mrs. Dobbs, said something about how nice Talullah looked, though she seemed to be trying to figure out why even as she spoke. The beehive and shag devotees asked, "Who did your hair?" She replied that Cindy had, as her Christmas present to the town. The other women nodded as if they could understand Cindy's need to do something about Talullah's hair as a civic project.

There were so many comments about her looks that she wondered how people had seen her before the trim. Tacky? Unkempt? She became a little impatient, and she braced herself for some insulting comment from John.

She didn't get to talk to him. On her way home she glimpsed Cindy standing and shivering on her snowy steps talking animatedly with John. Cindy had obviously seen him walking past and had run outside to call to him. John was laughing. He had a nice laugh. Cindy was flirting. Poor Pat. Cindy was making her move.

Talullah drove on past and was surprised when she found herself frowning at the snow, feeling dissatisfied. How strange. Why should she feel that way?

John didn't see her new haircut until the night before the Christmas play. With that marvelous voice, he was the narrator. The dress rehearsal went so smoothly that it terrified everyone. Everyone knows that if a dress rehearsal goes smoothly, the play will be a disaster.

John talked to Talullah during a break. He didn't react to her appearance at all. Everyone else told her that she was a perfect Christmas fairy. She had on a long slip, lots of gauze, and a sparkly cardboard cone with a net veil wrapped around it to trail down to the floor, and she carried a painted dowel covered with sparklies and tipped with a tinsel star.

Cindy was on the makeup committee, and after finishing with Talullah, she frowned as she said, "You ought to use a little makeup. Tonight no one will know you. They'll all think you really are the Christmas fairy."

One of the second-grade elves said, as if on cue, "Ohhhh, she's a fairy princess!"

But John didn't appear to notice any change in her at all. He said in a serious undertone, "I never thought, Talullah, that I'd live to see the day you'd parade around a church in your underwear!"

She gasped.

"Didn't you know we can all see your slip just as plain as can be?" His eyes were twinkling wickedly.

That was his only reaction. He didn't say she looked like a fairy princess, or ask what she'd done with herself, or anything; he only commented on her being in her slip. His remark just showed what drew his attention. She looked down at her spare figure and decided that not even in a slip could she look bold. She looked perfectly decent. She gave a dejected sigh.

John had declined makeup for the rehearsal, but on the night of the play Cindy reserved him as her own project. By chance Talullah caught a glimpse of Cindy working on John's makeup, and she paused to stare. Talullah had never seen anything so erotic in her life, even though she'd devoted one entire summer to the soaps.

Cindy had her hand behind John's head to steady it, and she worked in apparent concentration, her lips parted, her tongue touching her upper lip, or her teeth gently gnawing on her lower one. And she must be somewhat nearsighted, since she had to be so close to him.

Watching Cindy work on John, all the other men laughed and became restless, but John was relaxed and patient. Oblivious? How could he be oblivious when everyone else was on their ear? Except for Pat, who was showing signs of hostility.

In the interest of peace Talullah felt it necessary to speak to John. Duty can be uncomfortable, as indicated by her blush, but if Pat should take exception to John receiving such close attention from Cindy, it would be embarrassing for it to happen in a church.

No one else appeared to notice the building crisis, so it was up to Talullah to solve it. She waited impatiently for the normally slow-moving Cindy to dart away to find another color on the supply table then seized the opportunity to hiss to John, "Pat is jealous; quit flirting with Cindy in front of him!"

John blinked and said, "Huh?"

"Be more businesslike." Confident that she

had straightened John out, Talullah flounced around and strode from the room.

Probably the best thing about a small town is that the inhabitants know everyone who's performing and don't expect much in the way of talent. Therefore attendance at town affairs mainly gives everyone free rein to comment during intermission, with a goodly supply of comments left over for the next day or two.

Although they winced, the audience sat still as Andrew attacked the piano during one break. He was a sickly child whose mother kept him alive on her will alone. He had no talent. In spirit he was a Huckleberry Finn whose body had betrayed him. When the piece had been...rendered, the audience smiled in relief and applauded his mother's determination.

They were equally courteous for Melody's toe dance. Her body was a collection of sticks that she balanced on her toe. That was an effort, and everyone held their breath, because she was quite uncoordinated. Her mother was also willow thin and another thwarted talent.

The play was satisfying, maudlin, cloyingly sweet, amateurish and familiar, with some eyebrow-raising talent here and there. One such was Talullah's. As with everything else, her emotions were completely involved. She was so concentrated on the part that she *became* the Christmas fairy. Her magic was believable. She had the best help from Squeeky Polgari, who was five. Squeeky was equally committed in her role as the Christmas fairy's helper, and she, too, believed. It was charming.

Through it all, John's marvelous voice wove a spell. And his subtle makeup was a work of art.

They all sang Christmas carols after the play then trooped off home through the snow. It heightened the holiday spirit.

When Talullah emerged from a basement dressing room, holding the cone hat carefully so it could be stored until next year and carrying the bale of gauze, she saw Cindy laughing with John. She was distracted only minimally as Benjamin touched her arm and said, "You did good."

As she started to smile in reply, his uncle roared from the stairs, "Benjamin! We're waiting!"

Benjamin turned and hurried toward his uncle, who reached out to grab his arm as he scolded the boy. All the while his wife placatingly gestured to her husband.

That scene was stored in Talullah's mind, the major portion of which was occupied with

Cindy's hand on John's arm and the fact that her full breast was brushing that same arm.

John called, "Hey, Talullah, you were a lulu!" Then he grinned at her. As she stiffly turned away, he said, "Wait!" But she pretended not to hear.

Talullah went on home, spoke to her waiting cat and climbed the stairs to her bedroom. She didn't feel the lift most performances had given her in her lifetime of participating in various plays and musicals there in Tarkington. She felt drained and strangely depressed. Perhaps she was catching a cold.

She took some vitamin C and undressed, but instead of immediately putting on her long flannel nightgown, she went slowly to her mirror to look at herself.

Except for the obvious accoutrements, she could pass for a teenaged boy of about fifteen. Her depression deepened. If she brushed against a man he'd never know it.

It had never before occurred to her to brush her body against any man's. Cindy did it with practiced art. She was really beautifully female. She left no doubt in John's mind as to her willingness. In spite of Talullah's censuring attitude toward such conduct, she felt envious that Cindy could do it so well—and that she was equipped to do it.

Talullah decided that if she really were the Christmas fairy, the first thing she would do would be to feminize her own chest.

How silly.

Why would she want…boobs? It was such an irritating word! She shuddered delicately. But why would she want an enhanced chest?

As she was, she didn't have to wear a bra. When she leaned over, she didn't have to worry about displaying anything…unseemly. She could run unhampered. Men always looked at her face. She sighed.

She would never marry. She had faced that fact some years back. She didn't need a man. She was self-supporting, free to do as she pleased, busy, involved. Why was she going along this same path yet another time? She'd worn it into a rut years ago.

She wanted children. That was what really hurt. She was a natural nurturer, but she had accepted the fact that she would never marry, so why was the idea intruding now?

The Matchmakers. They'd raked up the whole problem again. And of all the impossible people—they'd chosen John.

How could he possibly be interested in her? He was such a superior male. He was gorgeous, good-looking, magnificently built, intelligent, sexy, perfect.

She'd known him forever. They knew each other so well that he could only see her as an unrelated sister. Someone who was too well known, dull, with no surprises. Men married women for sex. And for meals. Not only was she not a gourmet cook, but look at her body. How thrilling…about as exciting as unadulterated mush.

Plagued by all that familiar, unsolvable stress, she got a headache. She needed to sleep, but how could she? She would go over and over the same old thing, and that would keep her awake.

She put on a velour robe and slippers and went down to the kitchen but, with her headache, she made do with the night-light and didn't turn on the overhead fixture. She got milk from the refrigerator and poured some into a pan to heat. Plain old warm milk.

Prissy had followed her down, and Talullah gave the cat a lick of butter. "I'm glad you're here," she told Prissy. The butter was a bribe to get the cat to stay. What sort of bribe could she give a man to get him to stay with her long enough to give her a baby?

People were more tolerant of illegitimate children these days, but even so, she wouldn't, couldn't, do that to a child.

Actually, she couldn't fathom doing...that... with any man. It seemed so...intimate. The very idea had always turned her off.

There was a tapping on the window across the table from her. She glanced up idly and there, framed in the window, oddly lighted...*there was the wolfman!*

The shock was instant. The nightmare from fifteen years ago had turned real! She stood up, and her chair crashed over, causing the cat to leap up and screech in surprise.

Talullah shrieked, too, and fled wildly from the kitchen, tore down the hall and raced up the stairs to the safety of her room, where she slammed and locked the door, leaving the cat in the hall. She ran to her window, pushed it fully open—it was on the opposite side from the kitchen—and leaned out to yell at the top of her lungs, *"The wolfman!"*

With her third repeat, the Morrisons' lights came on. Then the Turners' lights, followed by

finally everyone else's. Paul's mother was the first
to come outside, wielding a broom, running with
flapping slippers, her bathrobe flying open, her
stout body thudding with every stride. Behind her
came Mr. Morrison, yelling as he ran after his
wife, trying to pull on a recalcitrant boot.

Flinging her arm sweepingly to one side, Talullah yelled, "That way!"

Mr. Turner joined the chase, and then two other
neighbors, and the hue and cry was heartening.
Through the telltale snow they tracked him down
between the Phillips and Adcocks houses. With
no leaves to block the view, Talullah saw it when
it happened. They caught him!

## Chapter Five

Talullah yelled out her window, "I'll call George!" George Townsend was the night cop.

But as she started to pull in her head, Mr. Turner called, "No!"

That made Talullah look outside again at the approaching knot of people, who were talking companionably and gesturing against the background of snow as if in a Brueghel winter landscape.

"You don't want me to call George? Who is it?" Talullah strained to see his features. The group appeared oddly casual. The wolfman was walking with them like an old friend.

"Don't call." Mr. Morrison's voice seemed amused. "It's okay."

Okay? What was okay about a wolfman prowling her neighborhood? She frowned at the separating group of vigilantes. One man even laughed out loud.

Calling good-night to Talullah, the group dispersed, leaving a lone figure, unmoving. The wolfman? They were leaving him there? She was ready to yell for them to come back when the wolfman said, "Talullah, you are a real pain."

"John?"

"Come down and open the door and give me something to drink. And what are you doing to your cat?"

She stared down at John Peal, who was the wolfman. How shocking. No one in his family had ever shown a tendency to do anything so bizarre. He had to be a throwback to his European ancestors. He probably had roots in Transylvania; that had been the cause of his...

"Talullah! Come down and open the door! Are you strangling the cat?"

She realized that Prissy was still in the hall and probably terrified. How often in their acquaintance had Talullah bolted up the stairs and locked her door? It had been confusing for the cat.

Obediently Talullah left the opened window and crossed over to unlock the door, only to be confronted by a cat who was as indignant as John Peal.

Ordinarily Talullah would have apologized to the cat and soothed its feelings, but she was in something of a trance. She continued on down the stairs, followed by the indignant animal, and went to the front hall to open the door to admit...the wolfman? Into her sanctuary? What idiocy was this?

With the cat still complaining, Talullah stood back as John entered the house. He began to shed his coat in something of a temper! What was going on? Had he tried to catch the wolfman and been thwarted? That had to be it.

He snarled at her, "Why did you screech like that?"

She replied tartly, "I was not screeching; I was sounding an alarm." John had always been irritating, she thought.

"It sounded suspiciously like screeching to me."

Just then his scarf fell from his pocket as he threw his coat over the newel post at the bottom of the stairs. As she tried to think of the perfect response to his critical words, she bent to pick up the scarf. It was crumpled, so she looked down at it to straighten it out and—it was *the wolfman's mask!*

She shrieked, and the mask seemed to cling to her hand.

"My God, Talullah, what the *hell's* the matter with you?"

By then her fingers had released the mask, which hit the wall and plopped evilly to the floor, and the cat was halfway back up the stairs. Talullah pointed, her other hand to her pale lips. "You found his mask."

"It was me."

"I."

"It was I."

"What was?" She turned enormous, scared eyes to John. "It was you at the window?" she whispered.

He moved impatiently as he said, in a very grudging way, "I didn't mean to really scare you. I just wanted to shake you up a little."

"You did."

"You were always so cool. Even as a little kid. It drives me nuts wh—"

"Obviously." She stretched out the word in a telling way.

They glared at each other. His voice grated as he said, "I need a shot of whiskey."

"I only have wine. Philo locked up the strong stuff."

"That figures. How about coffee?"

She stretched her lips in an insincere smile and replied, "Of course." Being hospitable to wolf-men is de rigueur.

He declared crossly, "You've always been a very irritating female."

"*I?*" She had to take two very deep, calming breaths. She was not going to become engaged in a shouting match with John Peal! She stormed down the hall into the kitchen.

The cat had her head through the stair posts, watching with large eyes and giving small, confined jerks of its head as she tried to keep tabs on the incredible behavior of the humans.

John stormed along after Talullah and said, "Yes, you! You are the most infuriating woman I know."

"Then pay attention!" she rounded on him, leaning forward from the waist as she said furiously, "The Matchmakers are trying to pair us up."

"Good God, Talullah!" He snorted impatiently.

It was obvious to her that he was as opposed as she. Maybe more so. She turned away slowly and bent down to right the chair she'd overturned in her flight from the wolfman. He took the chair from her grasp and straightened it. She went to the counter to measure coffee into the coffee maker.

They were silent. He sat in the retrieved chair by the small round table with its centerpiece of miniature poinsettia plants in a clay pot. She brought a cup and saucer over to the table and set them by him. Then she took the glass of milk she'd abandoned earlier and poured it back into the pan to reheat it.

He watched as she did all that. And he considered the overturned chair and the milk glass and said awkwardly, "You didn't give me time. You were out of here like a shot! I was taking off the mask. I really didn't mean to frighten you, Talullah."

Tears were clinging to her lashes, so she kept her head turned away. "I know. It's like the snake."

He was a snake? "What snake?"

"You told me you had a present for me at nursery school, and I held out my hand and you put a snake in it."

He saw her wipe her hand down her robe, as if she could still feel the snake on it.

"I couldn't have done that."

"It's very similar to wearing a wolf mask and tapping on a window."

He sighed. Then he tried to soothe her. He said reasoningly, "Talullah Baby...."

And she screeched! He gasped, startled, as she turned on him. He rose in astonishment to confront the catamount that whirled toward him, and she swung her fist at his jaw—very ineptly. As he moved instinctively away, he had to put his hands out to save her from falling.

She was briefly still as she drew in a breath to realign her attack, and he said informatively, "You ought to go down to Brian's gym and learn self-defense. You could break your wrist hitting someone that way...if you connected. But you telegraph your punch. Anyone could see it coming a mile away."

She finished taking in that deep breath and, without exhaling, she took in two more as her eyes flared dangerously.

He appeared surprised. "You're angry!"

"John Peal! Go home!"

"I haven't had my coffee."

"Good grief."

"Look, Talullah Ba—"

"Don't you *dare* call me that!"

"I don't know what's set you off. I've apologized. I've been reasonable and you're flying around screeching." He rescued the milk, turned off the burner, and poured the liquid into her glass. He poured his coffee and eased her into the chair opposite his.

"You don't see anything wrong with standing at my window with a wolf mask on? You think that's normal behavior?"

"It was dumb." His face candid, he continued seriously, "I only meant to startle you. I thought you'd think it was funny. We talked about the wolfman not long ago. I had a hell of a time finding a mask this long after Halloween. I had no idea you were so high-strung." He frowned at her. "You always seem so calm. I've always tried to joggle you out of it."

"I can't believe you."

There was a long, very silent silence while the clock on the wall hummed efficiently. Finally John said, "The coffee is great. You're a good cook." That was followed by another long silence while he contemplated her. "You have to know I would never harm you."

"I used to have nightmares about the wolf-man."

"I used to go out at night trying to find him."

"How could you? How old were you? Weren't you afraid?"

"His appearances at Tarkington windows went on periodically for some years. My friends and I were about twelve when we first started looking for him. We figured it had to be someone who was bored. Who was trying to stir things up. It was probably Buddy Fremont."

"Him?" She was astonished. He was a harmless, clownish man who had been dead ten years or so. "Why do you think it was Buddy?"

"First, there haven't been any sightings since he died, and…"

"Other than tonight." Her voice was heavily laced with sarcasm.

He gave her a patient look before he said, "We caught a glimpse of him one night when we were prowling, looking for him. We chased him and he laughed. He had that funny laugh, remember? High and wheezy."

"And you deliberately went out looking. How could you?"

"There were four of us." He said it as if that explained everything.

She suddenly thought of the cardinal and all the sparrows.

It was after one when he left. He stood in her vestibule and shrugged his coat onto his shoulders. "Are you all right now?" he asked.

"Of course."

"Not scared?"

"No." Her voice was solemn. He'd stayed all this time to comfort her? To make her feel secure again?

He looked down into her face for a serious minute; then he bent his head and kissed her lips very gently. She was so surprised that she didn't even kiss him back. He lifted his head and looked at her. Then he said, "Good night, Talullah-lulu." He went on out the door, closed it after him, and made a lot of noise walking across her wooden porch, down the cement steps and crunching off through the snow.

She leaned her forehead against the etched glass door to watch him walk away, and she wondered how many of her neighbors were doing the same thing before taking a look at the clock to note how long he'd been there.

He'd forgotten the mask. It was still lying by the wall. She didn't think she could bring herself to touch it. What an incredible thing for him to have done! To deliberately find a mask in order to scare her to death. To come over to her house after the play...why hadn't he gone with Cindy? She'd certainly been available. Maybe Pat had objected?

Prissy came along and was elaborately startled by the dormant mask. She hissed, the hair rising along her back as her tail bushed. Prissy was really very dramatic. It probably came about because she was alone so much that she had resorted to drama in order to entertain herself.

Instantly Talullah recalled how she herself had behaved so recently, leaning out the upstairs window, waving one hand and screaming. No, she had not screamed; she had only called "Wolfman." She considered her conduct with detachment and knew she had not been dramatic.

She said to the cat, "It's a mask. That's all. Quit being eccentric."

The cat hissed at her, too, and went up the stairs in great bounds then paused at the top and looked back. She probably had to pause in order to catch her breath after all that effort.

Talullah went up the stairs with more dignity than the cat had. She left the mask lying on the floor, where it had fallen. She went into her frigid bedroom and closed the window gently. Then she turned to the bed in time to see the cat push her nose under the comforter and wiggle herself in after it. Naturally that put Prissy in the middle of the bed.

Talullah took off her robe and laid it aside then lifted the comforter and crawled in, buffeting the cat, who dug in and tried to keep the middle share of the bed. But Talullah was used to cats and held her own against Prissy, so she managed to get her share of the bed…to start with.

In the morning, when Talullah awakened, she noticed that Prissy had her neatly blocked in one upper corner of the bed and was curled under Talullah's knees so she couldn't move.

Her phantom lover had come to her in the night. Having chased the wolfman away the phantom again turned into John Peal. Then John had argued for…an intimate reward. It was very embarrassing. She had blushed and sputtered. How could she ever do…*that* with John Peal? The opportunity…uh…the necessity would never arise, because John would never try to do anything. Even the phantom John Peal would only have claimed his reward so he could snort and laugh when she gave in. It would have been so humiliating to have her own dream laugh at her.

She dressed absentmindedly and put on a yellow sweater with cinnamon trousers then tied her newly shaped hair at the back of her head, but she used a yellow ribbon to do it. She looked so pale after last night's Christmas fairy makeup—and, of course, from lack of sleep—that she even used a little blush and touched her lips with a little gloss so she wouldn't appear too sickly. Then, with her lips that nice color, she had to add just a smidgeon of golden eye shadow.

That morning, still full of their theatrical triumph of the night before the kids were wild. She finally made them put on their coats and boots and ran them outside and around the school twice before she took them back and got them to settle down and apply themselves to math.

It was when they took off their coats the second time that she saw Benjamin's eye. It was discolored. And into her mind came the clear replay of his uncle angrily grabbing Benjamin's arm. Had he hit Benjamin? Talullah's heart turned over. Surely not.

Bobby had a split lip, and she frowned. Then she asked almost hopefully, "Benjamin, did you and Bobby fight?"

"Naw."

She couldn't ask... Yes, she could ask Benjamin. "Did someone hit you?" She held her breath. Child abuse was rampant these days. And Benjamin's uncle *had* spoken to him harshly.

"Naw," Benjamin said tiredly. "I fell." But he couldn't look at her.

Alarm ran through Talullah. That was what child abusers always had the children say.

"Did someone…push you?"

"I slipped."

Talullah didn't believe it for a minute. She turned to Bobby. "And did you slip, too."

"No. My brother hit me back." He laughed in good humor.

That was believable enough. The brothers tangled all the time. Out on the playground, at school. On the street going to and from school. Bobby and his brother Tim cheerfully beat the tar out of each other at every opportunity.

Benjamin didn't have a brother, but he did have an uncle who spoke crossly at him and grabbed his arm. Talullah felt very quiet inside and decided she would talk to Mrs. Dobbs about Benjamin.

That was also the day she caught Bobby smoking during recess.

John "just happened" to be outside the school that afternoon, wearing jogging clothes and a stocking cap, looking absolutely, sinfully attractive. He grinned at Talullah and asked, "How'd it go? Any wolfmen tapping on your windowpane? Anything exciting happen today?"

Just then Bobby came along, hell-bent as usual, and ran into them as his brother branched off and ran on past, making rude noises.

John swung Bobby around and held on to him. "Hey," he scolded the boy. "You're too old to be running into ladies. Tell Miss Metcalf you're sorry."

He grinned. "I'm sorry, Miss Metcalf. How's your hand?"

"Better," Talullah replied primly.

Undaunted, Bobby told John, "She caught me smoking and knocked it out of my hand. She burned her hand, and she cried." He ended up with a rather serious tone.

John started to speak, but Talullah said quickly, "I cried because you were idiotic enough to smoke. It can harm you!"

"Naw, my dad smokes and he's still alive."

"I will speak to your father," Talullah replied formally.

With a depressing lack of fear or chagrin, Bobby said, "Okay. See you tomorrow." He started away then stopped. "I hope your hand's okay.'' He waved carelessly and was gone, to be joined by his brother. They played and tangled on down the street.

Talullah sighed tiredly.

"Let me see your hand," John commanded in a husky voice.

"It has a bandage."

"Why didn't you just tell him to put it out?"

"He's *ten*. I was appalled. I just wanted to get the filthy thing away from him...like a snake!''

Her reference to snakes went right over John's head. "All kids smoke sometime along the way. You did, too."

"Only that once, to see what it was like."

"That's all Bobby's doing."

"This isn't one time."

"There's nothing worse than someone who's reformed."

"You don't think I should stop Bobby from smoking?"

"You'll do as you see fit. Just don't panic. It's mostly experimenting. Boys tend to do that sort of thing."

"There is a limit to the things a boy should experiment with. Chemicals, for instance. Remember Mark Bartel? He lost two fingers trying to make that rocket."

"That was dangerous. This is just smoking."

She gave him a telling glance.

He held up both hands, as if to ward her off. "But, Teach, I saw the light! I quit! I'm reformed! I'm pure now."

She just watched him, and into her mind came the pictures of Cindy brushing against him as she did his makeup for the play. How pure was John?

"Are you walking?" John asked.

"Mm-hmmm." She was still distracted by the thought of Cindy and John's purity.

"I have to cool down; I'll walk along with you."

"You'll raise the hopes of all the Matchmakers," she warned.

"It's camouflage. They'll think you've hooked me and won't pay any more attention to me."

They walked in silence for a while; then she blurted, "If you had a student in a class and he appeared with a black eye—a little more than that, really; his temple is discolored, too—and you suspect his uncle is a stern man, and you wonder if there might be child abuse, what would you do?"

"First time?"

"He said he slipped."

"Benjamin." John made it a statement.

"Yes."

"Has he ever shown any evidence of abuse before this?" His tone was casual.

"No. But I haven't looked for any. He's very quiet."

"His mother died last summer," John said thoughtfully. "There could be other reasons for the quietness. He could be having trouble adjusting to living with his uncle Bill and that bunch of little kids."

"Shall I talk to Mrs. Dobbs?"

"Why don't you talk to Benjamin's aunt first? Say he's very quiet in school. How's his work? Is it okay?"

"Reasonable, comparable to last year's."

"That's a good sign. Talk to his aunt first."

"There's so much in the papers and magazines about child abuse," Talullah fretted.

"Remember Tom? Everyone knew his father beat him. No one knew what to do. At least now we pay closer attention."

"It makes me sick to think of it."

"Is that why you're so pale?" His voice was husky.

"No, some wolfman kept me up too late last night." She gave him a prim look as he laughed. He *had* kept her awake, both as a real visitor to her house, and as a phantom in her bedroom. Thinking that, she blushed.

He watched the blush and smiled, amused by her. "Are you going to invite me in for coffee?"

"Coffee isn't good for you, either." She mounted the steps to her house.

"Are you just going to go on inside and leave me out here in the cold? Talk about abuse! Do you think you could spare me one small glass of water?"

She considered it aloofly, then said, "I... suppose so."

"The ever-gracious hostess."

"And you can take that wolfman mask home with you."

"Maybe you ought to keep it. If I take it home, I could be tempted to wear it again." He deliberately gave her a wolfish smile.

She turned unbelieving eyes his way, and he laughed with absolute delight. She frowned and opened her door, and he trailed in as if he were welcome.

She went straight to the kitchen and filled a glass with water then turned and handed the glass to John. She still wore her coat, gloves and boots.

"Your welcome warms my heart."

"Hurry up."

Leisurely he relished the drink. "Ummm. There's never any other water that's so satisfying as the water in your own hometown."

"I wouldn't know."

John finished the last of the drink and put the glass on her counter as Prissy stalked into the kitchen. John said, "I was thinking of your cat after I left here last night, and it came to me what it looks like." He waited, but Talullah did, too. He went on. "It looks like a dog-pound reject."

Talullah looked down at the cat, who sat returning their examination with an expression very similar to John's. Talullah bit her lower lip, trying not to smile, but the laugh bubbled up and she couldn't restrain it.

John grinned, very pleased, and said, "Agreed?"

"Shhh. Shame on you."

"Let me see your hand." John's voice was soft.

"It's okay." She peeked up at his serious face.

He took her hand in his and slowly peeled off her glove before he removed the bandage and examined the burn. Then he did an absolutely outrageous thing. He cradled her hand in both of his as he lifted it to his mouth and gently kissed it.

# Chapter Six

She didn't see John for several days. In that time she never actually caught Bobby smoking. She did lean her nose fractionally in his direction and sniff significantly as she gave him a narrow-eyed look. But he turned wide, innocent eyes up and said, "The whole house smells that way."

And Benjamin healed. There were no new bruises, but how much of a kid does a teacher see in winter? Hands and face. And he was still so subdued.

Then, as she walked home one day after school, she saw Cindy driving John's car. Cindy honked as she drove on past, and that stopped Talullah dead in her tracks.

Cindy was driving John's car.

That was almost like a declaration. No man allowed just any woman to drive his car. It was so personal. And Cindy was driving John's.

So? What difference did that make to her? She didn't want John Peal. But there she was, standing there, staring off down the snow-rutted street, watching John's car disappear, knowing that it was being driven by…Cindy Bates.

Eventually she did start walking again. She ended up downtown, when she'd had no intention of being there, and she felt as cold and bleak as the weather. She stopped in Mr. Hooker's drugstore to warm up, and she looked so pitiful that Mr. Hooker *gave* her a cup of coffee. Mr. Hooker wouldn't give away the time of day, but he gave Talullah a free cup of coffee!

"John's been sick all week," Mr. Hooker boomed. "Caught cold, out jogging around like an idiot in that colored underwear he calls a sweat suit. Looks like long johns to me. If he'd been wearing something sensible, like he should have been doing, he probably wouldn't have a cold."

"John's sick?"

"Terrible cold. That new female doctor's been over there, holding his hand. And Cindy Bates. Seems to me he's not all that sick, just stretching

it out, enjoying himself. Man would be crazy not
to take advantage of two pretty women giving him
all that…attention.''

John was sick! Last week he'd met her outside
the school and walked her home in his jogging
suit. He'd wanted to get warm and asked her to
let him inside her house for coffee, but she'd only
given him a drink of water! And now he was so
sick that he had two women hovering over him.
If she'd just gotten him warm…

''Looks to me like the buzzards are after your
man.'' Mr. Hooker lifted his brows and gave her
a censuring look.

''John Peal is not *my* man.'' Talullah raised her
own brows right back.

''Oh?'' He made it a very disbelieving sound.
''That so?'' He wasn't at all convinced. Then he
looked around the drugstore and said knowingly,
''Gonna be lots of matchmakers disappointed in
you, Talullah Metcalf. You're not paying attention!''

''They might even learn to mind their own
business.'' She straightened her spine.

''They've been giving Cindy the rough side of
their tongues.''

But she retorted, ''It's none of my affair. Cindy
and John can do as they please.'' Talullah began

to realize the coffee hadn't been from the kindness of Mr. Hooker's heart. It had been a trap so he could talk at her about John. Well, two could play at this game. "How are your bunions today?"

She got to sip the rest of the coffee in peace. Mr. Hooker wasn't cut out for intrigue. He could be distracted.

All over downtown there were Christmas garlands of years-old, rather ratty tinsel. Stores had cotton snow on the other side of the glass separating it from the real thing. There were aluminum stars pasted around. And the fir on the square was decorated quite beautifully.

Then, too, the houses were festive, some with electric candles in the windows or wreaths on their front doors or lights strewn through the shrubbery. People were already calling Merry Christmas in spite of the fact they would be saying the same thing to one another just about every day for weeks to come. It was quite nice.

And in that spirit, Talullah told herself, she bought a small poinsettia down at the greenhouse and then, with an inward smile, exchanged it for a Christmas cactus, which she took to John's house.

He opened his door and glowered at her. He was in a bathrobe that was rather carelessly tied, and he needed a shave. He looked rough and masculine, and a strange shiver ran through Talullah's insides.

"Where've you been?" he asked in a grouchy way.

"I'm on my way home from school," she said through thin unsmiling lips. Then she added perfunctorily, "I'm sorry you've been ill."

"Why didn't you come over before this? I could have been dead."

"I only just found out."

"When you didn't see me around, you could have called."

"Why? Because I was the only woman not here?" She gave him a cold look.

"Oh? You heard about the others?" He smiled a little.

"Yes. And I see Cindy is driving your car." Her voice sounded prickly and accusing.

He turned away to hide his pleased expression. "It needed a valve job, and this seemed a good time to get it done." Then he turned back and asked, "Aren't you going to ask how I feel?"

She looked at him. He looked bigger in that small, untidy house. Her house was more in proportion to his size. He dwarfed this one. He looked so…untamed. It was a little frightening to be alone with him. He seemed so unrelentingly male.

She was still standing there in her coat and boots. She was becoming very warm, but she told herself that was because she was in a heated house dressed for the out of doors winter weather.

She said in a thin unsteady voice, with a strange swallow in the middle, "You look…fine."

"No thanks to you. I could have been buried yesterday for all you cared."

"John…"

"Talullah, I think we ought to get married."

"Mar…m-ma-ar-r…?"

"Married." He frowned at her, his hair messed up, his beard shadowing his face, his hands in the pockets of his robe, his hairy legs naked, his feet stuffed in old sneakers that weren't tied.

"Married?" Her thin voice had gone up three octaves. "You don't *want* to be married. You want to finish out your years as a rake."

"I'm thirty-one, a very vulnerable age for a man. Women are getting serious about settling down, and there aren't too many free men at this age. Most are taken. So I'm being besieged. My walls are crumbling…"

She could see he was a writer.

"...I'm about to be breached."

"Put into trousers?"

"Talullah..." He glowered and gave an irritated blast of impatient breath.

"So Cindy is driving your car."

"Hal called while she was here. She volunteered to pick it up for me."

"How sweet." That didn't sound sincere.

"I'm terrified that she's going to back me into a corner, and before I know it, I'll be married."

"You can decline."

"I've tried that, and she came over with chicken soup. Won't you marry me? Cindy would be miserable with me."

She protested, "We've known each other like brother and sister all our lives. We don't even get along!"

"It'd be perfect," he argued. "You'd protect me from predatory females, and I'll be your protection from everybody's interference. With us married, the Matchmakers would leave you alone. I hear you swore off marriage right after Pete—"

"That fiasco..."

"Well, I know what it's like to want everyone else to leave you alone and quit matchmaking. I thought we could solve each other's problems."

Then, feeling that she needed a little more convincing, he said, "I find you less annoying than most women."

"How flattering."

"You could think about it. If you were married to me, there wouldn't be any danger of a wolfman at your window." He smiled, looking excessively dangerous.

"No, not outside—but *inside!*" She thought frantically how to refuse and blurted, "I know about sex," she lied impulsively. "And I don't want to do it again."

He shifted his stance as he thought rapidly, assimilating the fact that she disclaimed virginity and declared she didn't want sex. He noted her stubborn chin and flung-back head. She was ready for battle.

He hunched his shoulders and frowned as he bit his lip. He read her quite well. "Talullah, let's wait a couple of days, and then we'll talk about it." His voice was gentle. "And thank you for the plant. It's very nice. What is it?"

"Uh…" She was so boggled that she couldn't think straight.

"Have I upset you?"

"No." Her voice sounded humiliatingly tiny and weak. Unsophisticated. She said in a strangled voice, "I have to get home. I'm glad you're better. Goodbye."

"Talullah..." He started toward her slowly, one hand out to gesture, his face concerned as he sought words. "Honey, I..."

"I'll see you in a couple of days. Goodbye, John." She whirled, snatched open the door and found herself on the porch as she pulled the door closed behind her.

The winter wind hit her like a spray of ice. She walked home in a daze. John had asked her to marry him. How incredible. Even more so was her saying she was experienced. Good grief! Her? Experienced?

She spent the rest of the evening walking around the house, arguing heatedly with "John." At times she almost agreed to such a marriage, but the rest of the time she was uncertain, scared. It was awful. The temptation was so intense. Marriage with John Peal? But such a marriage! Could she—should she—snatch at it?

At her request Talullah saw Bobby's father the next day. He was over six feet tall and about fifty pounds overweight. He was a good old boy, Yankee style, and he was easy and good-natured. She told him Bobby was smoking.

"I'll tan his hide," he offered pleasantly as he turned out one big ham hand as if offering the ultimate solution.

"Ross, if you didn't smoke, Bobby wouldn't."

"Now, Talullah..."

"If you love Bobby, and I know you do or you wouldn't be here, you'd quit smoking and be a good example."

"Geez, woman, you gotta be kiddin'." He shifted in the chair, making it creak in protest.

"He's ten years old, and he thinks it's neat for him to smoke because you do it. He admires you, he sees you as his idol."

"His idol?"

"He talks about you endlessly."

"What's he say?" Ross turned cautious.

"He talks about how you feel about things. You're a fine man, Ross. He loves you very much."

"Yeah. He's a good kid. Him and Tim. Both nice kids. They wrestle a little, and Betty worries about that, but me and my brothers did that, too. No harm in it." He paused, and then he smiled. "Idol, huh." He nodded, trying to minimize his grin.

Two days later John called Talullah at seven in the morning. His calling at this time confused her a little, and she questioned, "John?"

"You didn't come by yesterday to see if I was recovering."

"Are you recovering?" she inquired obediently.

"Yes. It's just a good thing I'm not a child; you'd make a terrible mother."

"You're a grown man," she began.

"But even grown men have to have some care. We'd all perish if it was left up to you. Then where would the world be?"

"A whole lot safer and saner."

"...and boring."

"Yes."

His voice amazed, he asked, "Did you say yes?"

"Yes."

"There's hope for you, Talullah-lulu. I'm calling this early to get my bid in for your evening. I can leave the house today, so I'm beginning my courtship. Miss Metcalf, will you do me the honor of having a small repast as my guest this evening?"

"Small repast?"

"I'm starved for McDonald's. I think my withdrawal symptoms are interfering with my recovering.''

''I see.''

''Then you'll go with me?'' He held his breath.

''Well, all right.''

''See? You can be civil to me! We're going to make this work yet! How about six o'clock, Miss Metcalf?''

''I suppose so. Shall I come by for you? It would be on the way.''

''No. We're doing this according to the book. I'll pick you up. Dress appropriately for McDonald's. I'll be there at ten to. And, Miss Metcalf, I am looking forward to the occasion.''

''Good grief.''

The punctual Miss Metcalf was almost late for school because she went frantically through all her clothes to find something suitable to wear to McDonald's with John Peal. Nothing was acceptable.

The only thing she found that she wanted to wear was a summer blouse. She couldn't possibly. But her clothes were all utilitarian. Sturdy cloth, quiet colors, serviceable. That summer blouse was yellow. Soft and feminine. But how could she possibly wear it in the snow just before Christmas?

She dug her best jeans and her yellow sweater out of the laundry bag and washed them, then put a note to herself on the door so she would be sure to put them in the dryer as soon as she arrived home from school. She viewed the chaos in her room and closet, closed her eyes to hide the untidiness of it all, and by then it was so late she had to drive to school.

How long had it been since she'd gone out with a man? She tried to remember. She'd only been asked out for a hamburger at McDonald's and she was on her ear. How ridiculous.

She didn't remember much about the day. She was nagged by the feeling that there was something she should pay attention to, but whatever it was eluded her.

That two-week school day was finally over, and she tried to hurry out, but it seemed that everyone wanted to chat about something or the other, all foolish things. She did finally get away. Then she hurried two blocks before she remembered she'd driven her car and had to go back for it.

She was in a dither getting the clothes into the dryer then efficiently slammed the door and listened to the dryer's patient hum, which actually managed to calm Talullah.

When the dryer was finally done, she grabbed

the sweater and jeans before she ran up the steps past the cat, who panicked, fled before her and went from the back of a chair up to the top of the hall cupboard to look down with wide eyes and distended pupils.

"It's okay, Prissy; I'm just in a hurry."

She went into the bathroom and turned on the water in the old-fashioned tub, which sat on claw feet in the middle of the large room. The tub was big enough for two, very deep and wide. The door latch was old and worn, so Prissy simply put her feet against the door and pushed it open so she could come inside and watch.

Deliberately Talullah opened the closet and pulled out the stool then climbed up to see the top shelf and study the collection of bath beads she'd accumulated over the years as gifts.

Sandalwood, gardenia, lilac, peach…peach? She took that one down and hesitated. Sandalwood? Wasn't Sandalwood the alluring scent of the South Pacific? The Oriental seductive one? Now, wait a minute, she told herself. Just what sort of nonsense was this? Seductive? With John Peal? Whatever was she thinking?

She took the peach over and tipped the fluted bottle into the water.

It did smell like peaches. Like summer. Maybe

with that scent she could wear the summer blouse. No, settle down, Talullah, and behave, she warned herself. She was only going out for a hamburger with John, whom she'd known all her life, and to whom she could not possibly appear seductive. If she tried, he'd rupture something laughing.

As usual, the cat walked the slick rounded edge of the tub, watching her. Prissy had only fallen in once and hadn't been too alarmed. But it was somewhat unsettling to wash oneself and have a cat walking around, fascinated, staring in critical interest. Talullah had never gotten used to it.

She bathed quickly and efficiently, emptied and cleaned the tub, dried herself and dressed. Then she went into her room and brushed out her hair, marveling at how nice it still looked after the trim Cindy Bates had given her. She started to twist it back, hesitated then brushed it free. She lifted a few strands and wound them around her finger then decided to buy an electric curling iron at the first opportunity.

With her curtain of brown satin hair, her face looked quite bland, and she cautiously put on a little makeup, surveyed herself then added a touch more, and agonized. Fortunately John rang the doorbell before she could take it all off.

He looked at her, a little surprised, and said,

"Hey, what did you do to yourself? You don't look half-bad!"

She bristled and her cheeks became pinker. He watched that and said carefully, "You look pretty, Talullah."

Stiffly she replied, "Thank you," but she didn't raise her eyes, nor did she smile. "Would you care to come in for a drink?"

"That would be nice." He, too, had become stiff, but that was the result of caution.

Awkwardly she indicated a bottle of wine and a clever cork remover. He handled that quite well. He looked at her to see if she'd noticed, but she'd been opening bottles of Philo's wine for years, so she wasn't impressed.

He mentioned bracingly that he was feeling better, and she said she was glad. He said it might snow, and she agreed. He asked her about Bobby's smoking.

Relieved that he had introduced a sensible subject, she replied, "I saw Ross Parker. I told him that if he'd quit smoking, Bobby would."

That made John laugh with such honest amusement that she wasn't offended. "You told Parker that?"

"Yes."

"He was probably smoking in the delivery

room as soon as he was born. There isn't any way in this whole world Parker could quit.''

''I told him he's Bobby's idol.''

''What a rotten, underhanded thing to do,'' John said admiringly.

''One does as one must.''

''You know,'' he said, changing the subject, ''this wine is great. And McDonald's...'' A look of pure bliss spread across his features. ''I'm sick of bland foods. Everyone brought me soup. I'm lusting for onions and garlic and *taste*.''

Instead of peach scent she should have hung a bag of garlic around her neck. Now why would she want to attract John's lust? She wouldn't. What she'd meant by that was...

''Are you ready?''

''Yes.''

They walked to the front door, where she reached into the closet for her coat. He had to hurry in order to help her with it. It had been so long since anyone had helped her into her coat that she turned wrong, then she put her arm up too high, and it was all very awkward. John was superb. He salvaged the whole maneuver, guiding her into the coat quite smoothly, considering that she was confused and unpracticed.

After that he simply took over. He held her arm

firmly, preventing her from helping herself. He
opened the door and closed it then helped her
down the snow-crusted stairs and into his car.

She so seldom drove with anyone else that she
couldn't prevent a little body English from coming through in response to his driving, and once
she even stretched her right leg out and "put on
the brake" when she thought he was approaching
a stop sign a little too rapidly. She wasn't even
aware that she did it.

He was amused and didn't comment. They arrived at McDonald's, but before the car had even
stopped he said, "Sit still. I'll get you out."

She did try to wait, but she felt so silly just
sitting there that she opened the door herself,
swung one leg out and almost slipped on the ice.
He had a strong hand ready, and didn't chide her
for not waiting as he closed the door.

Molly Lambrey was taking orders. Her eyes lit
up when she saw them, and she became very an-
imated and grinned widely. John didn't appear to
notice, but Talullah cringed at the imminently
humming Tarkington grapevine.

John escorted Talullah to a window seat and
divided their order. As he sat down, not across
from her but right next to her, Talullah whispered,

"Molly will be on the phone now, spreading the word."

"She's become an evangelist?"

"About us."

"What have we done?" He looked at her, shocked. "Is my fly open?"

Talullah choked.

John grinned and whacked her on the back.

It had been too much to suppose that John would conduct himself with dignity. Indiscreetly he greeted other people and treated the whole episode as quite ordinary. Why did she feel it was extraordinary? Just because she had been out of the dating circle for years didn't mean anyone else would consider John's taking her to McDonald's an earth-shaking episode. She was being hyper and really ridiculous.

Then she saw the Millers leave. A minute later she glanced out to the parking lot and saw the Millers tag the Caldwells, then watched as they gestured and exclaimed and then pointed—right to where Talullah was sitting with John.

"Why have you suddenly gone scarlet?" John wanted to know. He spoke quietly, in a low, teasing voice. "What in the world is going on in your wicked little mind? Are you planning my seduction?" he asked in pretended shock.

"The Millers just left and told the Caldwells we're here."

"Why should that bother you?"

That was true. Why should it? "I don't know."

He said solemnly, "Because you are planning my seduction? Being an experienced woman, you've decided, why not?"

"No." She had to wait until she had safely swallowed before she said, "Behave."

"I'm not the one blushing," he told her solemnly, controlling his amusement.

"John, you idiot."

"I'm completely over my cold, so you can safely kiss me."

"I never kiss on the first date."

"First date? My God, woman, I've known you since you were in diapers!"

"How completely unromantic!"

"It's very romantic! My ability to endure you has survived diapers, no teeth, and braces. You've never actually revolted me."

"I can't tell you how thrilled that makes me."

"I understand. Just sit still until the waves of titillation recede. I won't say anything else exciting until you regain control."

Talullah laughed. She put down the last of her hamburger and bubbled with merriment. John watched her as he grinned, his blue eyes electric and laughing.

"Are you in control again?" he inquired.

"Yes. Sorry about the slipup."

"You're susceptible to me." He nodded tolerantly. "This proves it." He watched her sputter as she tried to think of what to say; then he went on. "Although you're susceptible, you do have control. When I came back to Tarkington, you didn't fall to the floor in a swoon when you saw me."

"Neither did you."

He scoffed, "Men never do that. Men are manly and hide their emotions and responses. Well, to some extent." His grin was quite wicked.

She blotted her lips with a paper napkin and kept her eyes on the debris on the table. He was going to kiss her good-night. He'd just warned her that he was going to kiss her! How long had it been? A long, long time. But tonight he would *really* kiss her....

# Chapter Seven

Talullah didn't actually assimilate any of the rest of the evening. She was waiting for the kiss that she knew was coming. John would kiss her. Her breath became shallow. She licked her lips as discreetly as she could, then she had to blot them so they wouldn't be wet if—when—John kissed her.

Good grief. What on earth was the matter with her? She was behaving like some Victorian maiden who'd never been kissed. Actually, the kisses she'd garnered in her early years hadn't been anything to remember. Not like those in romances, with their shivers and quivers and borderline madness.

This kiss could be that way. John was going to kiss her. Her soul would soar, and her senses would go wild. He would lose control, and his desire would be on fire.

Interrupting her mental wanderings, John asked, "Have you tried it?"

She turned her dilated eyes to his and was shocked. Well, of course, she'd told him she was no longer a virgin. She asked, "What?" to give herself time to figure out a cool reply. If she wasn't a virgin, then of course she'd "tried" it. Why would he ask…?

Bemused by her, John repeated, "Have you ever tried chili powder on popcorn?"

"No." She was still wide-eyed and very serious.

John wasn't sure what she was thinking, but hers was an odd reaction to a discussion of popcorn. "I probably make the best popcorn in the universe." He acted elaborately modest.

She carefully watched his mouth. It was very masculine, chiseled, mobile. He had the faint beginning of laugh lines around his eyes. She looked into his blue, blue eyes. He watched her looking and was silent. She was so involved in studying him that she was completely unconscious of what she was doing.

He was very nice looking. His eyes were beautiful jewels. His lashes were thick, surprisingly so for a man. His daughters would have lovely eyes. He had a nice forehead. His hair was thick and springy. It didn't exactly stay in place. It mussed in an attractive way.

His ears were perfectly shaped, and the lobes were velvety. He would look great with a golden pirate earring. She wondered if he would wear an earring in this day and age. He had a nice nose. Strong and male. She'd never been attracted to a nose before, but his was perfect.

She knew that the Moors had deliberately made one flaw in each of their intricate, gorgeous designs because only God could make perfect things. God had made John.

From behind the counter Molly watched John and Talullah as they studied each other in silence, and she smiled and kept glancing at the clock. She was waiting for break time, so she could call her sister, her aunt, her cousin, the Morris clan, the...

John saw golden lights in Talullah's brown eyes. They were the reflections of the lights in McDonald's, though he didn't know it. All the rest of his life he would think she had golden glints in her brown eyes because of that night.

He smiled faintly at her serious study of him

and wondered what she was thinking. She was so interesting, so different. He wondered who had slept with her and been so inept that he'd made lovemaking distasteful to this sensitive, precious woman. He hated that man.

The walls she had built around herself were high and thick. He was still astonished that she hadn't turned him down with disgust when he'd so clumsily presented the idea of actually getting married. She'd even come with him for a hamburger after he'd clearly told her that he was beginning to court her.

He would have to be very careful with her. He would have to heal her from her first, obviously distasteful sexual encounter and see to it that she was carefully wooed. With the scope of her emotions she would be a hell of a lover, if he just didn't go too fast.

He decided on the oblique approach. With her distaste for men, it seemed the wisest, most unthreatening way. All he had to do was to be patient and careful. He could ease in closer as he gradually built up her trust until she relaxed. After that he would teach her to love him.

He smiled into her serious, upturned eyes. He licked his lips, and she watched in fascination. Then he smiled again, and she was hypnotized by the sheen on his lower lip, and she licked her own. He swallowed rather noisily, and she jerked her eyes away from him and glanced out into the snowy night then moved a little to show that she was alive and aware of where she was, as if she hadn't actually been off in a sensual world of her own.

For what seemed to both of them like an endless time, they dawdled over their sundaes, but finally they left McDonald's and went to his car. Because he was quick he managed to open the car door before she did, and he helped her into the passenger seat.

As they drove to her house, he said, "This is my first time out since I was sick, and I've got to get to bed early. I've enjoyed your company, Tallullah-lulu." He cast a smile her way.

"It's been very pleasant." She was as stiff as a pole. Her face, her lips, her body, all frozen.

Did she dread his kiss that badly? he wondered.

She was halfway out of the car when he got around it to her side. He managed to take her arm as he closed the door.

In nervous haste she stammered, "Would you...would you like to come in for coffee?"

"Rain check?"

"Of course." Was it relief that made her voice that faint?

"There's going to be a new film on at the Palace this weekend. Would you like to go with me?"

"Well, I suppose so."

"Good. I'll say good-night, then."

"Thank you."

"You're welcome, Talullah." And he leaned over and gently brushed her lips, hardly more than a butterfly's touch. He lifted his head and smiled into her disappointed eyes. Then he said, "Good night," turned, and left.

She stood in her doorway and watched him head down the steps and the walk, and get into his car. Then she went inside, closed the door and locked it. She had expected this to be the first real kiss John had ever given her, and it had turned out to be a complete zero.

She could have wept with disappointment. She'd been ready to melt against him, like a romance heroine. She assumed that "melt" meant to relax against him and not worry about touching. She'd been all ready to do exactly that. And he'd given her that cautious nothing kiss.

Was he a virgin? That didn't seem possible. Paul had said the West Coast women loved John.

Could he be…? No. Maybe he simply wasn't attracted to her. Maybe it was just as he'd said: they might as well marry for mutual protection from predators. A marriage of convenience. She wanted the real thing. She wanted the loving and caring and passion and children. She wanted it all.

How surprising! She did! She wanted it. What an astonishing metamorphosis. She had been perfectly contented with her lot. Then John had said they should marry—for convenience—and that he would court her by the book…and her whole plan of life had apparently collapsed! She had simply turned up her old maid toes and surrendered to the idea.

But if he didn't like her enough to kiss her better than that, what hope was there for them in a marriage? She wanted to know what it was like for a man and a woman to make love. What if he gave it up, and they actually did have a marriage of convenience?

She went to bed with a cold cloth on her forehead then lay awake trying to figure out what on earth she could do.

She would be an old maid all the rest of her days. She looked bleakly ahead at the years that would be her future.

A bleak future? She had never before considered that her future would be bleak without a man. She had been perfectly happy. Then John had to come along, and the Matchmakers had decided they should marry. How indignant she'd been! How irritated! She'd even told John to watch out.

And now here she was, disappointed in his friendly kiss, anxious that he liked her enough to make love to her and marry her and give her children. If it hadn't been for those blasted Matchmakers, those interfering busybodies, her life would have continued smoothly and serenely. Damn.

She would have to be very careful and not scare him off. How did women handle this sort of thing?

Now wait just a minute! Was she at all certain she wanted to get involved in this whole operation? Her life would be turned upside down. She would have to consider John's schedule, his meals, his clothes, his work, his personality and quirks, then perhaps children and all their complications. It would be very different.

What would it be like to share a bed? It was bad enough trying to share it with one small cat. A man would take up more room than a cat. Perhaps John would sleep in another room?

What had happened to her ordered life and

mind? Turmoil. Men only caused problems. And that nothing kiss…! If he couldn't do better than that, marriage wouldn't be worth the effort.

It was a long time before she slept.

Later that week Talullah met with Benjamin's aunt Sue, and they went for a cup of tea and a talk.

"How is Benjamin adjusting to living with you and Bill?"

Sue asked, "Why?"

"Is there trouble?"

"No. Not especially. Of course, Benjamin was an only child, and it's very difficult with three little cousins in the house."

"What about Bill? Does he resent another child?"

"What's the matter? Is something wrong?"

"Benjamin is so quiet. Then he had that black eye…."

"He said he fell…. You don't think Bill hit Ben? He never would! But he does feel Ben should have some discipline. No one had told Ben to obey for five years, and then it was only suggestions in his mother's soft voice. And after she died, we were so grateful he could come to us that I was too lenient. That doesn't mean Ben's unruly or backtalks; he just does things in his own time. Bill thinks he should be more considerate of others and adjust to living with the family schedule. It's been tough on all of us, but Bill would never abuse him.'' Sue paused then exclaimed, ''My God, you can't think we abuse him!''

''I didn't know. I needed to find out. Do you know of anything else that could be bothering Benjamin?''

''He doesn't dislike living with us. He gets a little irritated about having to do chores according to schedule, but he doesn't seem to resent us. Naturally he still grieves for his mother.''

''See if you can find out what else could be upsetting him. I do appreciate your being so nice about this. But I had to be sure.''

''I'm glad you asked me.''

The next day Ben's uncle went to see John at his house. John opened the door and said, ''Well, hello, Bill, come on in.'' He could see that Bill was agitated.

''I don't know how to tell you this, John, but I don't beat up on little kids.''

''Glad to hear it. Tell me about it.'' He took Bill's coat, and they sat down.

''That old maid...''

"She's going to be my wife, so that eliminates that title." John's face was serious.

"I've never been accused of beating a kid before," Bill said harshly, "and I don't know how to wipe that out of her mind."

"There was no accusation, only an inquiry. She's concerned. She doesn't want any kid to be miserable. There's something about Benjamin that worries her."

"I wouldn't hurt him. He's my own brother's boy! How could I hurt a child of his?"

"You would rather have Talullah ask about abuse than ignore the possibility, wouldn't you?"

"Well, yes."

"Talullah's a good teacher. She loves kids."

"She worries about Ben. Why?"

"He's not adjusting well. Talullah needed to know if there was a problem."

"I'll talk to him."

"We're on your side, you know."

Bill smiled a little, but he shook his head slowly. "When Sue told me that Talullah had asked if I hit Ben, it about made me sick to my stomach."

John reported his conversation with Bill to Talullah that evening, and she replied, "So that isn't it. What could it be?''

"We'll just have to find out what's going on.''

At his words a strange thrill went through Talullah. He'd said "*we'll* just have to find out,'' as if her problems were his, too.

He took to jogging during the time the kids went to and from school. He wanted to keep an eye on Ben.

When Talullah came home from school a few days after that, he was in her backyard, splitting wood for her fireplace. She took him a tall glass of iced tea and sat on a log to watch him work.

"You didn't have to bring me tea.'' He smiled at her.

"I knew you'd be thirsty.''

His eyes warmed.

She saw that he was sweating, and she asked, "Should you be working this hard after being sick?''

"It helps me sweat out my frustrations,'' he replied quite seriously.

"Oh.'' She assumed then that his book probably wasn't going well.

When he'd finished the tea, he put the glass down before he told her, "Benjamin's problem is a gang of kids. One is about his age, and the others are younger. They gang up on him.''

Into Talullah's mind came a picture of the sparrows with the cardinal; then she thought of John and his friends searching for the wolfman. Numbers against one.

John offered, ''I could just happen along every morning and evening until the gang gets tired of trying to get to their victim.''

''Let's talk to Sue and Bill. I think maybe I have an idea.'' And she told him about the birds.

Ben's uncle's initial reaction was, ''We'll find a gang for Ben!''

It took a while to slow Bill down and wait for him to decide that gang against gang wouldn't solve anything. They contacted the parents of the gang but they all said, ''It's just kid stuff. Let Ben handle it.''

Ben's uncle and aunt couldn't allow Ben to be beaten, so the only alternative was retaliation. But Benjamin told them solemnly, ''My mom said I should never hit girls or kids littler than me.''

It was his uncle Bill's kind voice that said, ''That's right. But a gang of kids against one changes things.''

Talullah wasn't privileged to see the confrontation the next day, but John did. The five kids

waited for Benjamin, and he didn't hesitate. He
kept walking. The gang began the harassment, but
Ben took out one of them, fended off another then
took that boy out with a shove—and by the time
he confronted the third one, he had the "gang"
in bawling flight.

The gang tried one more time that afternoon.
Again Ben did exactly as his uncle Bill had instructed, and again Ben sent them off crying.

That made the gang back off. They didn't attack Ben physically. There were catcalling insults,
but those could be ignored.

The problem seemed to be solved.

On the Friday night before Christmas week
Talullah was braced, because that was the night
she was slated to go to the movie at the Palace
with John. She really didn't know what to expect,
or what she wanted. She was undecided over
whether she was doing the right thing in seeing
John socially, as a date, to be courted by him.

She wore armor: a gray turtleneck, with gray
flannel slacks, and boots. She wore her hair pulled
back and went without makeup. She was reserved.

John was cheerful when he came for her. "The
movie is *Rocky Mountain Wolfman,* so I figured

you'd rather not see it. We could watch HBO on my TV.''

Fighting an odd sense of disappointment, she said forlornly, ''There's nothing on HBO that I'm eager to see.''

''How about going to the arcade and playing the machines? I'm really pretty good…and Fritz needs the business.''

''I find the games senseless.''

''Excellent practice in hand-to-eye coordination.''

''No. Thanks.'' She did tack that on.

''I'm not healthy enough yet to tackle ice skating on Peterson's pond, or even a moonlight walk through the snow. Did you know it's snowing again?''

''In time for Christmas.''

''Will you come to my house for Christmas?'' he asked nicely.

''You're roasting a turkey?''

''Why not?'' he asked. ''I'm a brilliant chef.''

''Didn't anyone invite you over?''

''I thought we might begin our own traditions,''John said easily. ''So, how about it?''

''Well, I was going to the Morrisons'.''

''They'll understand.''

''We could have dinner here.''

He looked around, pleased that she'd offered, and delayed his acceptance so it wouldn't appear that he'd baited the trap for her invitation. "That would be perfect. You've decorated your house very nicely. It's pretty."

"It's just family things from the Christmas box in the attic. All very old."

He decided that now was the time. He took a piece of mistletoe from his pocket and looped its string through the entrance hall light fixture. Then he stood under it and said elaborately, "Oh, look, mistletoe!" before he reached out and slowly drew her close to him.

She was a bit resistant and stiff, even somewhat irritated. He ignored all that and pulled her closer. He was bigger and stronger, and obviously determined. She might as well get it over with, she decided. Another nothing kiss. She'd survive it.

He kissed her. It wasn't at all like that other kiss. He put his arms around her and held her close to him, and he seemed to be trying not to crush her. It was very strange, and it caused her insides to shimmer oddly. Then he looked into her eyes with such a comforting look, as if they were good friends.

She relaxed a little, and he hugged her to him without doing anything else. Just a really nice, friendly strong hug. She relaxed a little more. His hands moved on her back in the most charmingly comforting way. Like an old friend. She felt the last of her tension leave her body, and she even put her hand on his shoulder. She could be friendly, too.

Then he leaned his head down closer, and she closed her eyes, waiting for the brief salute he'd given her last time. Finally his mouth touched hers. It was very pleasant. She moved her lips to briefly return the kiss, and his mouth moved a little in response.

A startling sensation surprised her knees. While she was experiencing that, his lips opened a bit and brushed hers, his kiss softer and—different. She gasped, and he took advantage of that and slid his tongue along her lip in a very disturbing way that caused strange and amazing things to happen inside her body. In her breasts, along her spine, and deep down in…down deep.

His hands moved on her excited spine, and her toes curled inside her boots. She had to have air, but she couldn't make her nose work properly, and her mouth had to help, so she pulled back a bit to open her lips—and the kiss turned into something absolutely astonishing.

He didn't thrust his tongue into her mouth; he

was smarter than to do that at this early stage in his campaign. But he softened his lips and moved them in a tasting, relishing, caressing way that wasn't like anything Talullah had ever experienced.

She clung to him, pressing against him with her arms and chest, but carefully arching her back so she wouldn't brush against him below the waist and give him any wrong ideas.

The kiss went on, and her response was intense. Her fingers were in his hair, but she was only aware of his mouth, and the fact that she had to keep her back bowed. That was hard to do with her knees in such a deplorable state.

When he finally lifted his mouth from hers, her lips stayed ready in case he wanted another kiss. He was thrilled—that is, on top of everything else she'd done to him. Her back was under his hands, and he longed to un-bow it and press her to him, but he resisted…this time. He smiled down at her.

She blinked several times, swallowed and said very seriously, "That was really…quite pleasant."

He made a deep, very sexual sound of agreement. Then he said huskily, "You have a very nice chin." That wasn't what he meant, but he'd needed to say something and that had come out.

"My chin?" She frowned, puzzled.

"I've always liked it."

"My *chin?*" She appeared to have trouble comprehending that.

"How about mine?"

Her eyes inspected his chin and she said, "Well, it's very cleanly shaven."

"My dad always said to me, 'John—' we were on first-name basis, and he always called me John."

She nodded seriously.

"'John,' he would say. 'Always shave.'"

"I like whiskers. When I was little, my daddy used to whisker us. My mother would coax him to do that. He thought she was silly, but eventually he would, and we'd squeal."

He was as solemn as she was. "Who would ever believe my dad could have been wrong?"

"I suppose there are times when you would have to shave." She trailed one finger gently down his smooth cheek.

"I suppose."

"I would like to watch a man shave. You don't use an electric razor, do you?"

"Not anymore."

She didn't even know exactly what he said. She was waiting to see if he would kiss her again. He knew that, and he was girding his loins to resist. She'd had enough for now. And so, for God's sake, had he! He really ought to let her go. He said, "If it was someone in Tarkington who made love with you, don't tell me who. Make up a false name. I have to know a name, though, or else I'll glower suspiciously at every man I see. I can't live that way. Who was it?"

"I must confess that I lied. I never tried it."

He was struck dumb and blurted, "You're still a virgin?"

She moved, and he reluctantly released her. His arms wanted to hold her, and his body needed to be close to her. He said, "Never?" And since that didn't really make sense, he added, "You never did it? Why not?"

"I pulled my hair back and wore glasses."

He scoffed, "And you think that put guys off?"

"And I was rude."

He watched her soberly. "Why?"

She couldn't tell him then. So she searched for a reason he'd accept: feminism. And she told him a true thing. "When I was an undergrad, I knew an absolutely brilliant woman who could have changed the medical world. Her mind was so quick and curious and open that she could solve the unsolvable. She was a genius.''

"She fell in love,'' he guessed.

"Yes. She just had her fourth child, and she may never go on with her studies.''

"One of her kids might go into medicine,'' he said, meaning to comfort her.

"They're all just like their handsome father, charming bubbleheads.''

"Even the baby?'' he scoffed.

"He bedazzled the nurse at birth. He'll be an undistracted womanizer.''

He kissed her again, but though he kissed her nicely, his mouth didn't coax her, nor did his hands entice her. It was difficult for him to control himself, to resist the temptation to try to arouse her again, but he did it. She *had* been aroused that first time. Yes, indeed she had. He smiled at her and said, ''Talullah-lulu, you're an anachronism.''

"Because I'm a virgin?''

"Um-hmmm.''

"There are more of us than you would ever believe possible.''

They settled down to a jigsaw puzzle and spent the evening quite pleasantly, except for Prissy, who liked lying sprawled on top of the puzzle and had to be removed from the table and then shut away in the morning room with the TV on for company.

"Talullah, you spoil that cat."

"I have to live with her, so I try to make things pleasant."

"Will you do that for me, too?"

She gave him a narrow-eyed look and inquired wickedly, "Lock you in the morning room with the TV?"

He only chuckled.

Why had he pulled back from the second kiss? she wondered. What if he didn't want her? What if...what if she agreed to marry him, and he couldn't bring himself to make love to her? What if he found he didn't want her at all, and he just simply...couldn't? What if she revolted him? He very well might not be attracted to slats.

And now she knew that making love might be very nice. The feelings his kiss had aroused inside her body were fantastic. Another kiss like that and she would have lain right down there on the floor and—she would have let him. Right there in the entrance hall on the rug Great-Great-Grandfather Phillips had brought back from Turkey. She would have—if John hadn't drawn back.

Maybe the kiss hadn't been nice for him. Maybe he hadn't been able to stomach the thought of another one. Maybe she revolted him. Oh, why had she ever gotten involved? Damn.

That night her phantom lover came into her room and removed his clothing before he climbed into her bed. She was breathlessly eager and sought his arms. He took her against his warm body and held her.

She almost lost consciousness, she was so thrilled. She moaned and strained against him. His low, deep voice asked what she wanted in the most lascivious whisper that curled her toes and sent a riot of sensation through her body. She held her mouth up, and he kissed her! His first kiss! It was all the miraculous things she'd ever dreamed of; it was exactly like that second kiss of John's!

She reveled in it. She moved her mouth and opened her lips as her body caught fire and her feverish hands moved on his bare shoulders. "Oh, my love," she whispered emotionally.

His arms loosened, and he drew back. She whimpered for another kiss, but he only patted her shoulder in a friendly way. She opened her eyes to plead—and looked right into John Peal's friendly eyes.

She lay in her tangled bed for a long time before she got up and straightened her gown and smoothed out the covers. Then she lay soberly awake, staring at the ceiling.

On Christmas Eve it seemed that everybody in town crowded into the tiny Catholic church for midnight Mass. It was the only church open at midnight, and attending had become a tradition, even for Protestants.

Bobby and Tim and their parents were there. Bobby whispered to Talullah, "Miz Metcalf, you have a boyfriend!"

Talullah replied primly, "We are acquaintances."

Tim asked his brother, altogether too audibly, "Does that mean they're shacked up?"

Talullah stiffened and pretended not to hear the snorts and coughs around them.

Then another kid, a little older, who was sitting in front of Bobby, defended her honor. "She's an old maid."

That silenced all the sniggers as people began to feel sympathy for Talullah. And that hurt worse. They pitied her. John had seen and heard it all. He allowed himself only a sideways peek at her stricken face, but he saw the tears that threatened to spill.

As they left the church everyone spoke gently to Talullah, and John held her arm close to his body and was sweetly solicitous of her. That brought smiles. Matchmaker smiles.

They went to her house for cocoa, and while they sat at the kitchen table dunking vanilla wafers into their cups to catch the melted marshmallows that floated on top, Talullah said emphatically, "I'd like to try it first."

John looked up, raising his eyebrows. "More sinfully melted marshmallows?"

"An affair."

He straightened, alert. "What?" He knew as well as he was sitting there that the only reason she'd mentioned it was that she'd been called an old maid by the kids. It wasn't the right reason. Quickly, before she went too far out on the limb, he said, "We really shouldn't."

"I'd hate to die a virgin."

"I can't believe you've lasted this long. How did it happen?"

"No one ever made love to me." There was a huskiness to her tone.

He fumbled along, trying to keep things light. "It's incredible. You're not bad looking."

"How kind." Her voice wavered.

Alarmed, anguished, he said, "No, really. I'm

not being kind. You're really very attractive. Nicely built. Good sense of humor. I've always liked you. Are you crying?''

"No, no. I'm just tired. It's late. It's Christmas. Joy to the world. I suppose it's just...after all these hundreds of years there still isn't 'peace on earth, good will toward men.'" She had done a good job of redirecting their conversation, she thought.

"That was peace between heaven and earth," John said helpfully. "God can't speak for peace between peoples."

"John, would you make love with me? Could you?''

He pushed his cup back, stood, scooped her up and carried her into the living room. There he sat in one of the big chairs, with her on his lap. He brought his hand from under her knees and laid it along her cheek, then kissed her. He slid his hand around to the back of her head and cradled it, then kissed her so gently that the tears rolled down her cheeks. He kissed those, too.

# Chapter Eight

Holding her sweetly, John kissed her temple, then asked, "Will you marry me?"

"Oh, John, you don't have to marry me just to save me from being an old maid."

"What are friends for?" He was still trying to keep things light.

But he shocked her. She'd asked him to have an affair; he'd countered with a proposal of marriage and suggested friendship as the basis. She became very depressed. What did he mean? She wondered if he was warning her that their marriage would be one of friendly convenience.

"I kill spiders and I open jars. I'm really very

handy. I've even been known to trap a mouse now and again.''

Talullah had never been around other kids that much. An only child, she had been isolated in a section of town where the residents were older, and children were only visitors. She didn't understand his kind of teasing very well.

It was her great-aunt Agnes and her distaste for men that had had the most influence on Talullah. Her aunt had been stridently independent, furiously antimale. She blamed men for all the troubles of the world. She'd rattle the newspaper and snap, ''Men!''

But Talullah was lonesome. She had always been a little lonely, really. And John seemed very nice. It was lovely to sit on his lap and have him soothe her. Perhaps it would be enough. There wasn't anyone else. Perhaps she could adopt some children. So, out of the blue, she inquired of John, ''Would you mind adopting children?''

They had been talking about spiders and mice, so he had to blink a time or two while leaping to the new subject. Adopt children? Of course, he realized. She wouldn't be able to face making love but she did want children, so she had decided to adopt. What a tangle. But he wanted her whatever way he could get her. He always had. "I like kids. If you want to adopt some, it's fine by me."

At least she didn't try to get off his lap. He was careful not to alarm her. His kisses along her cheek were very chaste. Those on her lips were soft and gentle. His eyes took only quick peeks at how lovely her body was curled against him, and how sleek and beautiful she was. After a peaceful silence, John urged huskily, "Marry me."

"Oh, John. You don't have to just because everyone is trying to force you into it."

"They are?"

"John…"

"Besides spiders and mice, I can solve other things," he coaxed unthreateningly.

"Wolfmen?"

"You're right! And I can reach things down from high places. I have all sorts of talents." He smiled and watched to see if she realized he was being sexy.

"I just don't know."

"It's after two, and I have to go home and put the turkey in the oven." He waited, because he expected her to move off his lap.

"I thought we were going to eat here?"

"I'll bring the turkey."

"John, about the affair..."

"You're the type who would be the statistical exception and get pregnant the very first time in spite of the array of prevention we could use."

"Would you...rather not?"

"Not now." He was being very careful. "Will you marry me?"

"If that's what you want." He had said nothing of love or caring or needing. Only friendship. Only convenience.

"You will?" He held his breath. If she committed herself, she'd feel obligated to see it through.

"Yes." It would have to be enough. "But I have to continue to teach. It's important to me."

"I understand. May I kiss you now?"

Good grief. Asking permission? "Yes." She closed her eyes and waited.

His breath was sweet and a little excited. That surprised her, and she opened her eyes to see what he was doing. He was looking at her body; was he disappointed in her? She wasn't attractive. She wasn't...womanly.

His gaze moved to her face, and for the briefest moment she saw a strange expression in his eyes that startled her. It wasn't friendly; it was...what was the word? But in that brief time his eyes turned bland, and he leaned over and gave her a controlled salute, softly touching her lips with his.

Disgruntled, she slowly got off his lap. She helped him with his coat and bade him good-night. After he had gone, she released Prissy from the morning room and they went to bed.

Had the look in John's eyes been...possessive?

Only hours later her grandparents called from Florida, chortling at being the ones to awaken *her* on Christmas morning. "How many times did you say it was morning just as soon as you could distinguish the outline of the windows. Did you get our packages? Do you have a tree? Why didn't you come down? It's lovely; the sun's out, and the temperature will be almost eighty today."

"It snowed last night. I miss you both very much. The packages arrived. Did you get mine? Merry Christmas." She said all the expected things, but she didn't mention that John Peal had asked her to marry him and she'd said yes. Why not? she wondered later.

She went downstairs and turned on the lights on the Christmas tree then made a Christmas wish as she'd done all her life. But she'd never had one come true. She had no hope for this year's, either. She considered the parade of wishes her grandparents had assured her would come true: that she would have a brother or sister; that her mother would return; that her father hadn't died; that John Peal would notice her; that she would be able to go away to school. That wish had come true, but it had been pretty certain before she'd wished for it. And she supposed the wish for John's notice had finally made it. He'd asked her to marry him. To save him from predatory females.

She wondered if that one fantastic kiss had been a fluke.

Talullah hadn't gotten enough sleep, and she was emotionally strained. She wandered around the festive house in a cloud of gloom. Had the look she'd surprised in John's eyes really been possessive? There had been such...fire. That really didn't make sense.

If he cared for her, if he wanted her, he wouldn't be so restrained, would he? Men weren't known for evasiveness in romance. They did control themselves, but to mask attraction would be unusually cunning for a man. A woman might, but a man wasn't that subtle. Though what did she really know about men?

But the look she'd glimpsed had been exactly the look she'd seen so many times in children's eyes when they'd captured something they wanted. In Prissy's eyes that time she'd caught a bird! How strange. She must have misread it. She was no prize. No one had ever wanted her. But then, she had never wanted anyone else besides John. She wanted John?

When the time difference was tolerable out in Washington State, she called Linda. There were shrill children's noises in the background, and she could hear Mark's laugh. At one point he called, "Merry Christmas, Talullah! Come on out!" And the kids shrieked something incomprehensible at her.

"Wish you were here, my dear friend," Linda told her.

"John Peal asked me to marry him, and I said yes."

"How perfect." No exclaiming, just pleased acceptance.

Impatiently Talullah replied, "You must remember we spent our lives fighting tooth and nail."

"You did the fighting."

"He was abominable."

"He'll keep you from being dull."

"Dull," Talullah repeated, as if she didn't quite recognize the word but found it distasteful just the same.

"I love you, Tal. I'm glad John has seen the light. Merry Christmas."

Disgruntled, Talullah was still sitting by the phone when the doorbell rang. It was only ten in the morning. A long day lay ahead. People would be dropping by all through the long day and she would have to put on a happy Christmas face and be kind. Ballooey. She heaved herself out of the small chair and went to the door. How would she greet John? He'd be carrying the turkey. That would eliminate the need for an awkward embrace.

She opened the door, and there stood Cindy Bates.

Positive, steam-roller Cindy Bates was fidgety and awkward. She thrust a foil-wrapped paper plate at Talullah and stood inside the door, but declined to take off her coat.

"It's cookies," Cindy said. "I didn't see John's car. Is he here?" Talullah shook her head slowly. "Good. I just wanted to see you. I watched you two last night at midnight Mass, and, Talullah, you two belong together. Even I can see that. John is very possessive of you. I'm backing off. I'm going to convince Pat that it was a last fling. He'll be willing to be convinced.

"I figure you were testing John. I can understand that. With a guy like that, with all the women who've chased him, you'd want to know if he's ready to settle down. If you've been worried about me, you can forget it. I'm no threat.''

"Oh, Cindy..." Talullah floundered.

Cindy smiled. "Merry Christmas. Those are Pat's favorite cookies, but this batch didn't come out quite right. Don't be alarmed; I threw two batches away. These almost made it." She grinned. "Gotta scoot."

And she was gone.

Linda had said "how perfect," and Cindy said they were meant for each other. It showed how far off the mark people could be.

She dragged herself upstairs, and Prissy watched with interest as she bathed, dressed in a red corduroy shirtwaist and made up her face a little rashly because she felt so bland and unholidayish.

She put two yams to boil, to be mashed and topped with marshmallows later, and she was making a relish tray when an unshaven John arrived.

"Merry Christmas," he said cheerily as he brushed by her, carrying a roaster toward the kitchen. "My grandparents beat my parents this morning in phoning, and they were unduly hilarious about waking me up. Why don't we take a nap? I'll never last out the day. Who is *that?*'' he asked as the doorbell rang.

It was Mike Morrison, who was in town for the family gathering at his grandparents' house. He was John's age and Paul's older brother. He'd come to deliver a plate of fruitcakes from his grandmother.

Mike greeted John briefly and latched on to Talullah. They went back to the kitchen, where Talullah fixed them each an eggnog, while John put the turkey into Talullah's oven.

Ignoring John as if he weren't there, Mike chided her, ''I thought you were coming to our house for today.'' The possessive ''our house'' wasn't quite accurate, since Mike now lived in Chicago. He had recently gone through a divorce.

She replied, ''We'll be over later this morning. I have gifts for your grandparents.''

Mike said softly to her, ''I'd planned on spending the day with you.''

At Mike's bald statement John turned slowly from the oven and looked at Mike in a very dangerous way that Talullah missed entirely. Mike looked back at John, not intimidated at all.

All he needed, John thought, was for some stud to interfere, confusing the issue and forcing his hand. He narrowed his eyes to emphasize his threat. Mike sat there at the small kitchen table, deliberately relaxing into a male sprawl and smiled just enough for John to know that he felt completely comfortable and not threatened at all. But then John smiled. His expression was so wolfishly anticipatory that Mike's smile faded back.

All this went on behind Talullah's back. Mike sat straighter, no longer trusting John to be civilized, and became a little belligerent because he'd been bested.

John didn't mind hostility. He did mind interference. He became bland and tolerant. Almost cordial. Mike loathed him.

Talullah had little to say, and John was barely civil, so Mike finally told Talullah he'd be back later. Then he gave John a look that said he had not yet abandoned the field. John smiled.

Talullah told Mike politely, "Tell your grandmother I'll be over later."

"We will," John amended.

"Yes," Talullah agreed almost absently.

Mike studied her, and as they moved to the front door, he stopped her under the mistletoe. It was then that he really looked at Talullah, and he altered his entire approach. Like John, he knew that, with Talullah, a man would have to be careful. His kiss was gentle and serious.

He lifted his head, his face earnest. "Merry Christmas, Talullah."

In a nastily sweet tone John asked, "Aren't you going to kiss me, too?" They'd grown up together and been friends; now they were squared off over Talullah. John's smile came back slowly.

Mike gave him a dismissive look as he told Talullah, "I'll see you later," and went on out the door.

John closed the door more firmly than he needed to. He thanked God he already had Talullah's reply. Mike would have been a formidable rival.

Talullah turned to go back to the kitchen, but John reached out and delayed her. He held her arms and looked up, positioning her under the mistletoe. Then he took his handkerchief from his pocket and wiped her mouth with gentle care.

Her look was questioning. He told her, "I don't want his spit on your mouth when I kiss you." He said it that way to make Mike's kiss sound sloppy and uncouth.

"He's really very neat and dry."

"Don't you like squishy kisses?"

"No. They're generally calculated, not reflective of genuine emotion."

He laughed.

"John, look at me. I have no figure at all. Who would want to arouse me? Who would want to make love to me? I'm not beautiful. I'm not sexy. I'm just Talullah Metcalf, spinster."

"You're engaged to marry me." He thought that would be enough to silence all her foolish talk, but he had underestimated the influence of her great-aunt Agnes.

He put his arms around her and hugged her to him, holding her; then he very gently moved his whiskery face along her cheek and down her throat. "Am I doing it right?"

"Oh, yes." She felt him trembling! Was he that nervous?

"I didn't shave this morning because I figured I'd give you a kiss today." He was being intentionally droll. They were engaged. Of course he'd kiss her.

But she thought he meant he wouldn't necessarily kiss her every day. Apparently he wasn't affectionate. He had changed. She could remember girls talking about him when they were young.

"Did it bother you that Mike kissed me? He's always been one of the crowd."

"Yes." He bit the word off because his tongue had replied without his permission.

"Are you..." She hesitated to ask if he was jealous; it sounded so possessive. "Are you jealous?"

He lifted his head so he could look into her eyes. "Yes."

"How do you account for that?"

He took some time to reply. He discarded the obvious answers and came up with, "Damned if I know."

She opened her eyes and stared.

He dissembled. "I can remember trying to pay Job Sommers ten dollars to take you to the street dance the summer you were fifteen. Laura Whitcomb insisted I do it myself. Do you realize that when we actually marry, Laura will be there— and cry—and tell everyone she's known for fifteen years that we were meant for each other?"

"Yes. She would say how many years."

"She said at fifteen that you were old enough to go to the street dance and that you wouldn't be able to get a date unless I asked you."

"Right." She sighed dispiritedly. "I was awful."

"Not really. You were kinda cute in a gangly, growing way...."

"You do have a way with words."

"But that was the summer that blonde was visiting Mary Beth. Remember her?" His low voice rumbled in his chest.

"I remember Mary Beth quite well; I had one of her kids in school last year."

"Not her. Do you recall that blonde?"

"Vividly." Talullah's tone wasn't particularly nice.

"I don't remember her too well, but she was something at the time. That was during the back to nature era, and she was about the only girl with makeup, and she had those big blue eyes and that blond hair...."

"Bottle blond."

"Was she? I was an innocent. But you were so *young!* God. Who wants to kiss a fifteen-year-old girl with braces?"

"You did."

"Did I really?"

He didn't even remember!

"How was I?" He smiled at her there under the mistletoe.

"I didn't know. You were the first, so I had no one to compare you to."

"Well, did you like it?"

"I really wasn't paying any attention."

"You *weren't?*"

She explained candidly, "There were the braces, and I was afraid my body would—touch yours, and I worried about saliva."

"And you didn't even notice my kiss?" He was a little indignant.

"You have to remember, you were almost seventeen and had been fooling around for—well, years!"

He grinned. "Who told you that?"

"Gloria, Beth, Tommie... They said you were an animal. So I had to be careful not to drive you amok by getting close or kissing too wet."

"You were so safe." His chuckle was delicious. "You've probably never been as safe as you were with me that night."

"What a caddish thing to say."

"That was then." But before she could ask what he meant by that, he went on. "Have you told your grandparents about us?"

"Not yet. I can hardly believe it."

"Believe it." He grinned down at her. "I told. I've told everyone. Your grandparents know."

He kissed her carefully, because he couldn't really handle more than that, and he could whisker her only a very little more because, although she refrained from squealing, she moved and gasped and about drove him crazy.

His gift was a ring. Talullah was amazed! "How did you get it so soon? You just asked me to marry you!"

"I plan ahead."

He had had one on hand? Why would a man who wanted to avoid marriage have a ring handy? "You mean you carry the ring around so in case you find a woman you can tolerate, you're prepared and that way she won't have a chance to change her mind?"

He reminded himself that he was pretending she would be his shield; he couldn't say he'd bought it after seeing the golden lights in her eyes at McDonald's, so he just said, "Yes."

He put the ring on her finger and kissed it. As her eyes filled with tears, he said gently, "Don't cry, Talullah Baby; we'll have a beautiful marriage."

She didn't even notice that he'd called her Talullah Baby. She gave him a packet of fine white linen handkerchiefs. They were ones she'd bought years ago to give to another man, but he'd broken up with her before Christmas. She had never thought there would be another man to whom she would give gifts. She had never thought the time would come when she would be engaged.

John used her bathroom to shave. From the top of the toilet tank Prissy watched avidly, fascinated. Very boldly Talullah leaned in the doorway. Watching John shave struck her as a very intimate thing to do.

After their Christmas dinner they sat back and smiled at each other. It, too, had been intimate. She searched for things to say. He wasn't aware that she felt a bit strange entertaining a man in the house alone.

They went to the Morrisons' and had Christmas cookies and fruitcake, and sweet, heavy Christmas wines. And everyone admired the cat's eye and diamond engagement ring.

"Cat's eye?" Mrs. Morrison asked John. "Why a cat's eye stone for an engagement ring?"

"To go with her eyes. The golden glints."

No one else could see them. But John knew they were there. He'd seen them at McDonald's.

Even the engagement wouldn't have stopped Mike. By then only a marriage would have made him pause, but his effort was too late. Talullah didn't even notice his attempts to attract her. And John wasn't encouraging at all, to say the least. He invited Mike out of his own grandparents' house and said quietly, "Lay off." And that nice, civilized man could just as well have had a club in one hand and been clothed in a skimpy hide tied around his waist, because his attitude was very primitive.

Mike had always been conscious of Talullah, but when he was younger he'd sought more exciting company. He'd married an exciting woman who hadn't wanted to settle down, who didn't want to give up flirting, and while she hadn't matured, Mike had. This time he wanted a different kind of woman as a wife. He saw women differently now. Talullah was his kind. But John had made his objections very plain.

Had Talullah given Mike any encouragement, had she so much as focused her eyes on him, he would have tried even then. But it wasn't John's implacable threat as much as Talullah's indifference that finally stopped Mike's bid for her attention.

Back at her house Talullah and John discussed where they would live. When they called the Metcalfs to talk about the wedding, her grandparents begged the couple to stay with them in the family home.

"You wouldn't mind?" Talullah asked.

"Seven months of the year you would be alone in the house while we're in Florida, and the house will be yours eventually, anyway."

"I'll have to ask John."

"He won't mind."

And he didn't. "That way we can keep a close eye on them while they're in Tarkington. And we'll have the whole upstairs."

Did he mean they would have separate rooms? Talullah frowned.

After Mrs. Morrison had actually seen the engagement ring, word spread like wildfire through Tarkington, and there was great satisfaction among the Matchmakers.

It was amazing to Talullah how placidly the townspeople had accepted the news. No one was astonished. No one seemed to share her amazement. That baffled her. No one else saw it as a miracle.

# Chapter Nine

That night, when her phantom lover came to Talullah, he came dressed, and he didn't take off his clothes. He walked to the side of her bed, wearing John Peal's face, and he smiled down at her kindly.

Talullah awakened to lie there in her spinster's bed and stare soberly at the night-darkened ceiling. It was an omen. While she and John might be intimate, they would have a friendship marriage. She would be trading her phantom lover for a friend. Her dreams of passion would remain just that—dreams. She felt tears ooze from her sad eyes.

John decided that there was no need to delay. They would be married on New Year's Day and "start the year right."

Talullah had no objections. The clothes she had would be adequate. It wasn't as if she would need to dress herself for a lover. There were no clothes that could enhance her clothes-hanger body.

They called their grandparents and all of John's family. They managed to get a notice in the *Tarkington Weekly* in time and called key people to pass the word. They actually called people! Redundantly. Everyone already knew.

The two sets of grandparents flew back from Florida into the snow and ice, and a limo with a driver and an attendant met them and spent the weekend carefully carting them around over the icy roads and walkways.

Phyllis even flew back from Italy. Her gray hair was a wealth of short curls. She was vibrant, slim and flat-chested. A free soul. Cheerful and filled with life, she relished whatever she was involved in.

Talullah was stiff with her mother, but Phyllis ignored it. She brought Talullah a smashingly gorgeous gown of white chiffon that was perfect for the wedding.

"Chiffon in winter?" Talullah was a stickler.

"With white fox." Phyllis had brought that, too. "I'm only lending you the white fox." She acted as if they were friends!

Phyllis gave John a beautiful, poster-size picture of Talullah that stopped up his throat with emotion. The picture had been taken by Harry, Phyllis's photographer husband. He had caught Talullah—aged seventeen—as she stood on a rocky outcropping to survey the Aegean. Her lips were parted as she first saw that fabled sea. Her hair was loose and wind-teased, and the breeze pressed her soft dress to her slender body.

It was more than just a beautiful portrait of a lovely young woman. In the pose of her body, the turn of her head, the expression on her face, Harry's photo had caught the woman. The spirit of her. The strength, the adventure, the wonder. It was Talullah.

Studying the picture, John said slowly, "Maybe when she sees this, she'll know at last."

"She *still* doesn't?" Phyllis asked.

"She will."

"Ah, John, what did I do to her?"

"It was Agnes."

"It was her father. He wouldn't let me take her with me. We had terrible quarrels over that."

"It'll be all right," John promised Phyllis.

"Once she sees the picture, she'll know how Harry sees her. Then she'll know you love her, and she'll begin to heal."

"She's a little hard to reach," Phyllis said sadly.

"It'll be okay."

"Doesn't she suspect it's a lovematch yet?" Phyllis gave a frustrated frown and shook her head.

"Once we're married, she'll have to realize my love for her, and then she'll recognize hers for me."

"Ah, my dear boy, this won't be easy. Don't rush her. She's such an innocent."

"I know."

Paul Morrison, being inadvertently responsible for the wedding, was best man. It delighted him.

Mark and Linda Redburn flew in from Washington State because, as Linda told Talullah, "You're one of those women who will stay married all her life, so I have to be there this time if I want to see your wedding." Linda was matron of honor.

The church was packed. Almost everyone there claimed to be solely responsible for the marriage, but they all agreed that the couple's timing was terrible. New Year's Day?

"Why couldn't you wait until spring?" one woman asked crossly.

"Or get married in February? Nothing ever happens in February!" another complained.

"Or sometime in the warmer weather."

"At least they made it early enough that we won't miss many of the football games."

When John and Talullah finally left the reception amid the rice showers—which caused her some cynical thoughts—John mentioned, "We'll still be able to see the West Coast games." Then they drove to John's house, where they would spend their "honeymoon."

They were tired, so John suggested that they wear their pajamas as they watched TV and offered to make some of his universally-best popcorn. He was very uncomfortable with the situation, which dismayed and amused him at the same time. "There will come a day when we'll laugh over this," he told Talullah very seriously.

She turned and looked at him, totally at sea. Why in the world did he think this farce was potentially funny?

Talullah changed in the second bedroom and fought back tears. She had thought that if she ever got married there would be breathless kisses and hot, eager hands. He was going to watch a football game.

She put her chiffon gown on a hanger and touched it with tender fingers. She'd felt beautiful in it, but John hadn't said anything. He'd looked at her long and earnestly, but he hadn't said anything. He was probably appalled by the step he had taken in marrying her.

She opened the door of the bedroom and walked out into the living room just as John came in from the kitchen. He stopped and looked at her. She was wearing a beautiful high necked, long sleeved, floor length nightdress. Only her face and the tips of her fingers showed. It was white and lacy. And modest. Very modest. She was so beautiful to him that she took his breath away. He said softly, "Somehow I knew you'd have a nightgown like that."

She looked down, her gaze unhampered in her view to her toes. "It has lace."

"Quite a bit."

She was still looking down at her toes and wishing she had breasts.

To break the awkwardness he suggested, "Come sit down on the couch. The game's started."

She said, "This has to be the strangest wedding

night of all time." Perhaps if he realized that it *was* their wedding night...

"Have some popcorn." He adjusted the pillows, making a place for her by him. He placed the popcorn on the other side of him as he glued his eyes on the screen. She probably had on a chastity belt under the Victorian gown.

"It's..." She hesitated. "It's our wedding night."

He grinned at her almost ruefully. If he weren't careful theirs would be the classic clumsy coupling of a complete novice and a man who wasn't as experienced as everyone thought.

He leaned down and kissed her very carefully. She didn't draw away, but she looked at him with such big, earnest eyes. She was a little scared. How could he survive? How long would it take for her to agree to let him love her? "We're married." He needed to remind them both of that.

"Yes. It is a surprise, isn't it?"

"I'm a little disgruntled."

She assumed he would now tell her that they would sleep in separate rooms and be good friends. He would make it clear.

He waited for her to ask why he was disgruntled, and when she didn't, he explained, "I had a lot of years left to be a rake.'' He grinned wickedly.

He was teasing! ''A rake? You clean gardens?'' Quite sassy for Talullah Metcalf…Peal! She was married to John Peal! Quite boldly she reached across his stomach for a handful of popcorn. Her hand was high enough above his body that—in ordinary circumstances—it wouldn't have touched him, but he was aroused. She jerked her hand up, looked down then looked at John's still face. Without thinking, she blurted, ''Why, John! How *nice* of you!''

That surprised him into laughter, and she watched him, baffled. He asked, ''Nice?''

''I mean…to *try.*''

''Actually, I wasn't trying.''

''You mean even *I* can set you off? How amazing!''

''Don't you know you're attractive?''

''Not very.''

''You're lovely.''

''You never said one thing after Cindy gave me that trim, and then there was my makeup as the Christmas fairy…''

''You don't need embellishing. Why do you suppose I'm in the condition I'm in?''

She asked, ''Do you…want to?''

"It's our wedding night." Didn't she share the wonder of that with him?

"Yes. I suppose it would be the logical time." She was sitting stiffly, her hands folded in her lap, her face averted.

Would she? Very gently he chided, "You certainly sound eager."

"I *am* curious," she admitted quite frankly.

He frowned. "You find me only a curiosity?"

"No, no, no. I think you must be one of the kindest of all men."

"How erotic."

She tried to figure out how kindness could be considered erotic.

"With you a virgin, Talullah Baby, this is going to take a while longer." He wanted desperately to love her, but he wanted her first time to be beautiful.

"Do we have to post the banns?" She actually smiled a little, but she blushed, too.

"We made our declaration."

She chattered nervously. "It was a shock when I was, oh, thirteen or so, and I realized the marriage ceremony was really an announcement that the couple was going to sleep together. No wonder brides blush! Everybody *knows!*"

His voice was slow and tender. "What about

the rest of the ceremony? The honoring and cherishing and caring?''

''Yes.'' Talullah smiled a little. ''But everybody thinks about the sex. When I was quite young, I remember reading a caveman story, and the couple just went to another cave. No marriage ceremony! I was shocked. Then they had babies! I couldn't see how that was possible without a wedding. It nagged at me. I thought the writer was stupid, saying they had babies when they weren't even married.''

''Lean back, Talullah-lula. Kiss me.''

Woodenly she eased back, and his arm was there to hold her against his side. He put his other hand up to turn her face to his, and she said, ''If you kiss me with…your tongue…I might gag.''

''It's not long enough.''

She giggled with humor, but mostly with nerves.

He was serious. He kissed her face and eyes; he nuzzled her ear. He had the beginnings of an evening beard and he told her, ''I shaved very early so I'd have whiskers for you tonight.'' Then he moved his cheek down along her ear as his hand started to unbutton the myriad little buttons some man-hating designer had contrived to drive a man mad. But she did allow him to undo them.

She sobered, tensed and gasped little breaths that drove him crazy. She said in a low, sad voice, "I wish I had breasts for you."

He opened her gown and looked at her small breasts with their pink nipples. "Beautiful. Look, they fit perfectly into my palm." Gently he rubbed his hard hand over her chest, and she drew in a startled breath as her big eyes widened. No man had ever been allowed to do that to her. "Oh, John..." she breathed.

He scolded her charmingly. "And you think you need big breasts to arouse a man? You silly, silly woman."

He moved his whiskers down over her chest cautiously, expecting her to stop him, but instead her back arched and her hand moved shyly to the back of his head.

It was then that he lifted his mouth and kissed her, really kissed her as he'd longed to. He was terrified that she'd pull away, but she didn't. She didn't open her lips, but her body made little movements as his tongue touched her lips. His kiss was sweet and loving...and very passionate.

He trembled with his restraint. His breath was harsh as he kissed her. Her fingers were in his hair, and he heard the swift intake of her breath and then a little cry. He was afraid he'd crushed her and tried to lift his head to look at her, but she objected with a moan and clutched him.

"Talullah Baby..." Even his voice shook with his passion. His hands were feverish, sliding along her back, holding her tightly as if to absorb her into himself. "I'm going to make love to you." It was best to warn her.

"Yesssss." The word hissed. He was going to!

He stood to tug her to her feet, then led her into his bedroom. He fumbled with his own buttons then simply pulled his pajama jacket off over his head, untied the trousers and let them drop. He ripped off the coverlet. "Of all days to have made the bed!" he exclaimed. "But I didn't want you to think I was a slob."

He turned to her and saw that she was still standing, immobile, wide-eyed, looking at him. "You're still dressed!" Then he realized that she was looking at *him*, and he blushed, thinking he must look gross to her, threatening. Why couldn't he have been more subtle? Had she ever seen a naked man? One who was as aroused as he was? "Oh, Talullah..." he said with compassion.

She thought he was beautiful. So marvelously made. More beautiful than Michelangelo's *David*. "Uh..." She looked down at herself. He'd already unbuttoned her gown. It didn't take much to get her arms out of the long sleeves, but she couldn't quite bring herself to let the nightgown just drop down off her. She clasped it together over her chest, looked up at John and blushed scarlet. Her body was so...unattractive.

"Let me see you." His voice was rough.

"Must you?" she asked in despair.

Huskily he told her, "You're beautiful."

"Oh, John." He was so kind.

"Please."

She allowed the gown to fall and stood still, half turned away, her head bowed.

"Ahhh, Talullah," he breathed. He walked to her and put his arms around her. She stiffened, but he just held her, hoping she wouldn't refuse him. He stood still to give her time to adjust to their nakedness, but he was sweating, and he shivered with his desire.

She moved away from him. He tried to prevent it, but she went to the bed to lie down. It almost overwhelmed him that she would be willing. He was so touched that his eyes filmed, and he whispered her name as he lay beside her.

With his mouth and whiskers and hands and body he courted her. He was sure she wasn't indifferent, but she kept her hands on his head, and she still hadn't parted her lips. She moved and gasped, but he wasn't sure if it was passion or shock.

It was like her to honor commitment and simply endure. He almost lost control when he realized she was ready. His muscles were rigid, his breath furnace-hot, and his hands shook. He was very careful.

Slowly he eased to her. She gasped as he moved above her, his arm muscles shivering with his control.

Her thin voice said in his ear, "I can hardly stand this."

"Oh, sweetheart, is it…that bad?"

"Oh, no. It's just that I'm having a hard time holding still."

He exhaled a growling sound of relief, and his voice was gravelly. "You can move if you…want to." He'd swallowed, ruining his casual sentence.

"I want to…" She couldn't continue.

"Do it."

She timidly put her arms around his shoulders and tilted her hips to press against him.

He lost control. It was just too much. He took her wildly on his ride, and what he experienced was like nothing he'd ever known before. Sated, breathing in harsh gulps, he leaned his forehead to hers, disappointed that he hadn't managed to control himself better.

He kissed her cheek and tasted tears. Was she crying because she was ashamed or embarrassed? A virgin who had endured him. He'd been so clumsy and fast. He'd meant to court her through the evening and make gentle love to her. Instead he'd taken her to bed and had no more control than a kid. Damn.

As he eased away from her, he felt defeated. He leaned over and smoothed her hair back from her cool face, wet with her tears. At least she didn't flinch from him. He kissed her very sweetly, and she even allowed that. "It's all right," he soothed her.

"Is that all?"

"Huh?"

"How long does it take before you can do it again?"

The joy in his laughter as he wrapped his arms around her was complete. How could he have been so insensitive? Very smugly, exuberantly, he asked, "So you want to do it again, do you, Tal-ullah-lulu? Just what is it that you want to do?"

"I want to do all sorts of things. John, I could shock you."

"Try me."

"How embarrassing."

"I won't mind."

She moved to be released, and he opened his arms slowly. She sat up, her body reddened where his hairy chest had roughened it in his passion. Her nipples were swollen, because her passion hadn't abated. She was beautiful. Her hair was in disarray, her mouth reddened by his kisses.

She sat back on her heels, her hand modestly on the opposite knee to shield her body a little. And she looked at him. He watched her looking and then he *knew* where she would touch him, and his body stirred with the thought.

"May I?" She smiled at him, but her eyes were solemn and her face was serious.

He could feel his blood begin to surge, and he, too, smiled as his body anticipated her fingers. How shy she was. His eyes filled with love, and he felt very emotional as he watched her.

But she reached out shyly, and she only touched his chest!

He waited. Was she going to be more subtle than he had expected? More erotic? Would she make him wait for her fingers to move to him?

She brushed the hair on his chest and smiled as she watched her fingers. "It's very erotic," she told him, her eyes finally meeting his.

He cleared his throat. "Is it?" Amusement flicked through him. She only wanted to touch his chest? "I think you're a little passionflower."

"Surely not."

"Why not?"

"I believe I could...lose control." Her smile was gone now, and her face was serious.

"Go ahead." He put his hands behind his head and grinned. Had they all underestimated Talullah Metcalf Peal? His wife. "You have my permission to do whatever you like, Talullah-lulu."

She caressed him carefully, her attention on what she was doing. "Why do you call me Talullah-lula? You called me Talullah Baby after I cried after the snake."

"You're a lulu. You're special. You are..."

She had lightly scraped her fingernail over his nipple, and now she leaned over and set her hot mouth on it. He lost track of what they had been saying.

"Do you feel that?" she asked curiously.

"Oh, yes."

"I liked it when you did it to mine."

"I did, too," he assured her.

"I do wish I had nice breasts."

"You do."

"I mean 'spilling out' ones."

"I'm a leg man, and your hips are just gorgeous and you have the nicest bottom I've ever seen, and when you wear shorts I have to put my hands in my pockets to keep from patting you, among other reasons. Talullah, your breasts are lovely."

"Not like Cindy's. Did you make love with Cindy?"

"I couldn't."

"No?"

"She wasn't you." Perhaps now they could get to the real reason for their marriage.

But Talullah dismissed his words. She said, "Don't tell me I'm gorgeous, and you're madly in love with me." She gave him a level look. "I'd never believe you. But if you wouldn't mind, perhaps we wouldn't need to adopt? Could we have our own?"

He blinked, then said earnestly, "I'll do my very best to help out."

"John, you're just so kind."

He sat up and lifted her onto his lap with an awesome display of muscle power. He kissed her then, as he had wanted to so often. He told her, "Open your lips."

"Remember about the tongue."

But he tasted her. He teased her tongue into

touching his, and her breath quickened. His hands moved, and she shivered, her slight breasts lifted as her nipples hardened with the waves of sensation that washed over her and through her.

"John, you amaze me."

"You knock me sideways." His voice was hoarse.

"Now, John," she cautioned.

He explained, "I feel very like the time you hit me with the hockey stick when you were about nine."

"You would barge right in."

"Did you ever dream then that someday I might have you in this position?"

She laughed deliciously and wound her arms around his head in absolute abandon. Her head fell back, and her hair slid down her back so the silken curtain touched his arms.

"I want you," he growled roughly.

"You do? We can do it again? I've heard there are different ways," she ventured.

"Let's just work on one at a time."

"The same old way?"

"One time makes you pretty sassy."

"I'm glad I'm married to you, John."

"Me too. Me too."

"Oh…John…"

"Don't you like that?"

"Yesssss." Her hands clawed at his shoulders; her head was tilted back, her eyes closed, her teeth clenched. "John…"

"Like this?"

"Ahhhh."

"Like that, do you?"

"Ummmm."

"How about that?"

"Ohhhh."

"And this?" But his breath was unsteady and his voice low and rough. His hands slid down and she gasped.

He moved, and she made noises that excited him. He schooled himself to be slower and pay more attention, but she wiggled and writhed and moaned, and her hands were never still.

A sheen of sweat filmed her body. She grasped at John frantically, wanting him to slow down so she could regain control, but she was going completely wild.

Every nerve was thrilled. Her entire being was focused on sensation, and she cried out almost as if she were protesting. Then John carried her into Paradise. To an unknown world. Finally she returned to earth after her beautiful experience, and she wept.

He held her, whispering comforting sounds, pressing soft kisses along her temple and cheek until she sighed and relaxed. And finally they slept.

# Chapter Ten

It was very strange to wake up in a man's arms. How marvelous. She saw the whiskers on his face, so she was smiling when he opened his eyes. "Good morning, Mrs. Peal. Did you sleep well, sassy woman?"

"I didn't dream of a phantom lover." She realized that he had no idea how important that was to her.

"You don't need a phantom; you have me."

"Yes." She smiled and rubbed her hand on his cheek.

"Are they too long for whiskering?"

"Just right."

"Let's see if I can still remember exactly how I'm supposed to apply them." He looked down at her body as he lifted the covers. "Beautiful."

"Now, John, you know you're not supposed to say things like that."

"I wasn't saying anything," he explained. "I was just thinking aloud."

"I have an itchy place right here." She moved her head and exposed her throat.

He applied his whiskers gently to her throat. She made a sound as if she were tasting something delicious. "And here." She indicated her shoulder, and he moved his face there. After a minute she said, "I don't itch there." He didn't reply, just moved his face down farther. "Or there! You're being adventuresome. Stop that, John—I don't itch there at all!"

He paid no attention. She gasped, "Why... John!"

He lifted his face and asked, "Want me to quit?"

"How mean of you to ask me that. I'll have to decide." He waited. She said, "It may take a while."

Wickedly he continued to wait. She said, "Do it again so I can see if it's okay."

He did, and she said, "This is a difficult decision.'' But she gasped in the middle of the last word and then was silent. After that she made sounds, but still no decision, so he continued his scratching here and there and started other innovations that didn't involve the decision with which she was struggling.

When she could speak again she said with some amazement, ''I can't believe I never tried this before.''

''It wouldn't have been anything at all with any other man. You needed me.''

''John, you must remember that we have never agreed on anything…before this.''

''But when we do agree it's pretty fantastic, right?''

''I must admit that you're a talented man. I had no idea sex could be this way. Think of the years I've wasted!''

''I mean it, Talullah; it wouldn't have been the same with any other man. It had to be with me.''

''Now tell me you were a virgin up until last night. Go on, tell me. Fake it.''

''I think I was.''

''John!''

''I honestly don't remember any other woman before you. I don't think I even kissed another woman. No, I can't remember one. Just you, Tal-ullah Baby."

"What about all those almost-dressed women who were with you in all those pictures?"

"Almost dressed?"

"Not one was really inside her clothes, and they all had great big...grins for you."

He lay back and chuckled very low and inti-mately. It sounded so sexy and so knowledgeable. It was as if he were right where he wanted to be, and with the one woman who pleased him. She smiled.

"Come here, sassy woman, and please me."

She was so inept. But since she always flung herself wholeheartedly into any project in which she was involved, she tried earnestly. "You're just so interesting."

Her eyes checked for his reaction as she de-voted herself to his enticement. He helped. She was still enticing him when they reached the ze-nith and floated free.

They showered—separately. She declined his offer to wash her back. There was a limit to how many new things she could do in a twenty-four hour period. They went over to her grandparents' home for breakfast, and to bid all their visitors farewell.

One by one, or two by two, their friends and relatives left, until they were finally alone in the big old house. John had seated Talullah on a sofa beside the fire, and he was next to her, with one arm around her and holding her hand. She didn't appear to notice, just accepted it as natural. Her eyes were sleepy and vague. That vagueness was remarkable, since her brown eyes were so dark that they generally appeared bright and wide awake when she lifted her eyelashes. Today they were anything but.

John was still a little edgy. He was excruciatingly aware of Talullah. He couldn't believe that she was there beside him, wearing his rings, and that she was his wife.

"Are we going to share your room? Or have you chosen one of the other rooms?"

"My room. Then I won't have to shift anything around. You can just find places for your things." She gave John a sly, amused glance as she waited to see how he'd take that no-help attitude from her.

He smiled. "It'll be worth the effort."

She blushed.

He suggested, "I probably ought to see your room so I can figure what all I can move in and what I'll need to pack away."

"There's room for your toothbrush."

"My shoes will go under your bed." He made that a telling statement.

She blushed some more.

He rose and tugged her to her feet as he commanded, "Come on, woman, show me your room."

Prissy met them on the stairs, wide-eyed, as if she expected them to do something outrageous. John said, "Boo!" and the cat fled.

"She lived here first," Talullah reminded him primly. "She has rights. Saying 'boo' is a no-no."

"I'll try to remember."

She opened the door to her big room and needlessly explained, "There are the dressers, the closets, the library table, the chairs, the occasional table, the rug, and several lamps."

"And the bed," John mentioned.

"By George, you're right!"

"And your bookcase."

She looked at it and gasped. She'd forgotten to take John's books out and put them in the library downstairs. There they were. Right there.

"You have all my books!"

"Yes."

"Did you read them?" He turned to look at her.

"Every one. You're fabulous."

He sobered at her words. "Why, Talullah, how kind you are."

"It's true. I thought so all along."

He went to her and kissed her. "I get to sleep in your room."

"Yes."

"I suppose it's too early to go back to bed?"

"Maybe not."

It was later when they went into the room where the gifts had been displayed, and again they looked at Harry's photograph of Talullah. John said, "Don't look at the sea, look at you. That's the woman you've become."

"That I've become?"

"Look at you. You're beautiful. Look at your interest and courage and sense of wonder. You are that woman."

"It was beautiful there."

"Look at *you*."

"It was a fluke. Harry took a million pictures of me. He had a little camera and just shot them silently without the little clicks or buzzes. Then he enlarged them and put them all over his studio.

He took one of me in a grotto and it won a prize. He sent me the money at school. It came when finals were on, and I bought everyone pizzas from my mother's Italian husband.''

It was the first time she'd used the word mother in reference to Phyllis.

"How did an Italian end up with a name like Harry?'' John asked.

"He was named for his mother's very English father.''

"Those foreigners.'' John shook his head.

With school back in session, Talullah returned to her classroom, and John moved his things into her room. She had cleared out a chest and emptied one closet. "You're making me feel welcome.'' He was tender.

"I had to do it,'' she explained blithely. "I hate to iron, and if you jammed your things in with mine, you'd crush them, and then I'd have to iron them. I'm practical, ergo the cleared space for you.''

"You're supposed to make me feel welcome.''

"Welcome.''

John set up a studio in one of the many bedrooms upstairs, and he settled in to work, but he took time to consider the events and the people who were involved in their lives, and one of them was his vibrant, amusing, intelligent mother-in-law. He was convinced Talullah had to forgive her, because she would be cheated if she didn't.

Phyllis had told him, "Don't rush her. She has a way to go before she realizes she's loved by you, loves you in turn, and that she's a treasure. Then she'll be ready to accept Harry and me just as people. She may eventually learn to love us."

He had replied, "I think too many people are being far too patient and giving her too much time to come about and understand how things are in her life."

"She loves you, John."

"I knew that long ago."

"But she still doesn't know it."

"She will. Paul Morrison gave me this miraculous second chance."

In that big house, with just Prissy for fascinated company, the newlyweds enjoyed their isolation. They laughed and played and teased, and they took a bath in that enormous two-person claw-footed tub and splashed a great deal of water on the floor and almost deluged the curious cat. John laughed, and Talullah scolded him.

John said, "I know, the cat was here first."

"And has some seniority privileges."

"But I have privileges, too. Like doing this, or this…or this."

"John, you are outrageous." But her voice was placid and amused, and she said, "Men are so different."

"Only where it counts."

"Do you shed? Molt? I don't know much about men, and it's never been easy to ask." Talullah said to him, "You're really quite hairy."

"I could shave it all off."

"No." It was a quick, tiny no.

She loved to put her hands on him and touch his hair-roughened flesh. He didn't at all mind her doing that. He was thrilled with her response to him, but he longed for her to realize that it wasn't simply sensuality, but that she loved him.

John asked that the poster-size picture Harry had taken of Talullah be put up in their room, and eventually Talullah began to look at the young woman in the picture. It was a revelation that the body consisted of more than just breasts or the lack thereof.

John would lie in bed and say, "You're so beautiful. Look at that sleek woman. You're so perfectly made…in mind and body."

"Beauty was important to Mother." She hadn't called her Phyllis. "I thought that if I'd been prettier, she might not have left."

"Mildred told me that the quarrels between your mother and father were over you. They both wanted you."

"They did? I didn't know that." She thought about it and was incredulous. It was too astonishing to believe. But she looked at the poster and tried to see herself as she looked to her mother. She still didn't really see herself, but it was a beginning. She wasn't simply remembering the Aegean.

Elaborately disgruntled, John told her, "When you finally understand what a woman you are, you'll probably become so conceited that I'll have to think of something to do to bring you down to earth." But he was putting her on her back at the time, and his lecture lost something of its intent as her laughter bubbled up.

That January they were both involved in organizing the February midwinter festival. It had just been created because there had been nothing to help the Tarkingtonians get through a northern February, so now the Peals had to struggle through the snow and ice to meetings dedicated to doing something about February.

They ran into Bobby's father, Ross Parker. "Heard you quit smoking," John said without mercy. "How're you getting along?"

"Don't ask." Ross gave Talullah a disgusted glance. He looked as if he were wearing his oldest son's clothing, because he had gained about twenty pounds.

Talullah couldn't let it alone. She advised, "Exercise, and diet."

John said "Good luck," hastily and pulled Talullah along, away from Ross.

But Talullah did manage to call back to Ross, "Bobby is so impressed."

"You're heartless," John scolded. "How could you tell Ross that Bobby is impressed with him?"

"He is!"

"I know, but now how can Ross start smoking again with Bobby admiring the fact that his idol quit?"

Talullah smiled.

"Your only saving grace is that you're sexy as all bloody hell."

"Really? I thought it was you."

"Well, of course..."

Just then Mrs. Hilton shushed their whispers as

the meeting started, but John was thoughtful. He paid no attention to the meeting as he considered their lives. Talullah was so easy with him now. They talked and teased and loved. However, in spite of all that, they were still separate people, even though they shared a name, a house and a bed. What would it take for Talullah to realize that they had a true marriage?

With the weather so mean, and the Ketricks living on the other side of town from the school, Sue Ketrick drove Benjamin back and forth, and he showed no other signs of abuse or injury.

The time was an idyll for John and Talullah. He had told her he loved her several times by then, and she had scoffed. "Just because I'm a willing woman? Love is more than that."

She didn't register his reply of "I know." But then she listened as he told her, "You're judging me still as a youth. I am a man."

"...a wolfman," she amended.

"Other than that."

She couldn't bring herself to realize that he might love her. And she was content with his sweet affection. She could love him with the fullness of her heart; it didn't matter if he loved her or not. He appeared satisfied with her. She simply thanked God that he wasn't indifferent or only a friend.

Her grandparents were still in Florida, but kept sending Talullah vague promises to be in Tarkington soon, perhaps by April.

With March and better weather, Benjamin came to school muddy and with a bloody nose. Talullah cleaned him up and asked him how it happened.

"They threw rocks." He was dispirited.

Troubled, Talullah reported back to John.

Two of the gang had resorted to throwing rocks. The parents were told again. They were both younger than Ben, and one was a girl. But the families said, "It's Ben's problem, and he's bigger than they are. Let him handle it."

John replied, "Ben isn't old enough to raise your child. You're bigger than he is; you raise him." That made the parents mad, and they slammed their doors and wouldn't speak to the Ketricks or to the Peals when they met on the street.

John was exasperated. "When did not speaking ever solve anything?" He began to seek a solution to the problem.

But Talullah was furious and fretted, "It's abuse! Abuse is just as intolerable coming from children as it is from someone older. Can't they see how terrible it is?''

The problem still wasn't solved, but at least by now Ben knew that his uncle and aunt loved him. Meanwhile, he was given permission to defend himself the next time it happened.

It was the end of March before the two kids again threw stones at him. Ben took off after them and caught one. The other deserted her cohort and fled. Then their parents complained. ''Ben's a bully!'' and ''He's bigger!'' and ''He's picking on kids who are smaller than him.'' His uncle Bill replied, ''Ben has our permission to protect himself.'' With that Ben was left alone. There were still taunting words, but no more rocks.

It was after that last incident that John met Talullah after school and they walked home. Talullah was pensive. ''People join together for many reasons, and it works…for better or worse.''

''Ben will survive,'' John said to comfort her.

But Talullah was troubled. ''The thing that bothers me is that both those families would call the police if someone were attacking them, but they don't think a child should have help from an adult. They said we interfered. That we were overly protective of Benjamin. Without guidance, how does a child learn proper behavior? Is street behavior the yardstick of conduct?'' Sadly, Talullah added what troubled her the most, ''It's too bad for the kids.''

''Yes.''

''You know, John, I thought you just came back to dawdle until Tarkington bored you. But you've really become involved with our town. And you backed me on this whole thing with Benjamin. You didn't say it was up to Ben to solve it himself, or for me to stay out of it. You backed me.''

''We're a team.''

A team. She relished the term. As the months passed, the mortar had crumbled away in her emotional walls of self-protection, and the stones had loosened and fallen one by one as Talullah's realization of love came slowly.

She had come such a long way from her prickly hostility to John when he'd first returned to Tarkington. She'd progressed from a physical longing for a phantom lover to the reality of love, from seeing John only as a facade, a false and shallow mask, to knowing the whole man. He understood when she was troubled, listened and gave his support. He took her problems seriously and helped to solve them.

She looked at John as he walked along the muddy street, and her heart filled to overflowing. He was such a good man. "I can't tell you how it touched my heart that you backed me with Benjamin, but I'm even more astonished that we're together. That you married me. Why me?"

And in that ordinary setting, walking along that muddy street in Tarkington, John knew it was time. He said to her, "Care for me."

"You want *me* to take care of *you?* John, you're seven inches taller, and you must weigh fifty or sixty pounds more—"

"I didn't say *take* care of me. I want you to care *for* me. I want you to hold me and cherish me the way you promised."

"All the women in the world want you."

"I want *you.* I want only you to love me."

"And make love to you." She smiled a little, still not sure.

"Make love *with* me."

She finally understood how serious he was. He meant it! She stopped there in the lovely mud on that beautifully gloomy, windy March day, and she looked up at him, as serious as he was by then.

He gently cupped her face with his big hands

as he said with exquisite tenderness, "I love you, Talullah."

How amazing. He really did. She asked hesitantly, "You want me to love you?"

"Oh, Talullah Baby, if only you could. I love you with all my heart."

"I believe I've always loved you, John. But with the snake, and even just lately the wolfman mask…"

"I was only trying to attract your attention!" He actually made it sound perfectly logical.

"Good grief." She managed to get that in before he kissed her, curling her toes and impairing her ability for clear thought.

Neither of them remembered getting home. They smiled at each other, and hugged and kissed and swung their hands, their eyes clinging as they laughed so foolishly at nothing—at everything.

They went up the stairs to their room, and Talullah stripped off her clothes and crawled onto the bed so she could watch John as he undressed more slowly, his eyes on her.

He was just like her dream. Her phantom. Her phantom lover had never been a contrivance of her imagination. It had been John all along. John.

She smiled and reached out her arms to him.

"I love you," she said, the words filled with the love she was confessing.

He came to her and took her into his arms, pulling her closely to him. "Tell me again."

"I love you." Her voice was a little wavery as all the stones of her defenses crumbled. She said the same words again and again—more easily each time, and in a variety of ways. With passion, with need, with ecstasy. And he replied in kind.

Their love led into their future; they could now explore all the facets of their lives. It was the beginning of their happily ever-after.

\* \* \* \* \* \*

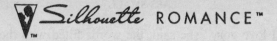

## *Silhouette* ROMANCE™

**What's a single dad to do when he needs a wife by next Thursday?**

**Who's a confirmed bachelor to call when he finds a baby on his doorstep?**

**How does a plain Jane in love with her gorgeous boss get him to notice her?**

From classic love stories to romantic comedies to emotional heart tuggers, **Silhouette Romance** offers six irresistible novels every month by some of your favorite authors! Such as…beloved bestsellers **Diana Palmer, Annette Broadrick, Suzanne Carey, Elizabeth August** and **Marie Ferrarella,** to name just a few—and some sure to become favorites!

Fabulous Fathers…Bundles of Joy…Miniseries… Months of blushing brides and convenient weddings… Holiday celebrations… You'll find all this and much more in **Silhouette Romance**—always emotional, always enjoyable, always about love!

SR-GEN

# WAYS TO UNEXPECTEDLY MEET MR. RIGHT:

♡ Go out with the sexy-sounding stranger your daughter secretly set you up with through a personal ad.

♡ RSVP yes to a wedding invitation—soon it might be your turn to say "I do!"

♡ Receive a marriage proposal by mail— from a man you've never met....

These are just a few of the unexpected ways that written communication leads to love in Silhouette Yours Truly.

Each month, look for two fast-paced, fun and flirtatious Yours Truly novels (with entertaining treats and sneak previews in the back pages) by some of your favorite authors—and some who are sure to become favorites.

## YOURS TRULY™:
Love—when you least expect it!

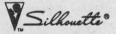

_Silhouette®_

# If you've got the time...
# We've got the
# INTIMATE MOMENTS

*Passion. Suspense. Desire. Drama.* Enter a world that's larger than life, where men and women overcome life's greatest odds for the ultimate prize: love. Nonstop excitement is closer than you think...in Silhouette Intimate Moments!

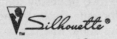

# SILHOUETTE® Desire®

Do you want...

**D**angerously handsome heroes

**E**vocative, everlasting love stories

**S**izzling and tantalizing sensuality

**I**ncredibly sexy miniseries like **MAN OF THE MONTH**

**R**ed-hot romance

**E**nticing entertainment that can't be beat!

You'll find all of this, and much *more* each and every month in **SILHOUETTE DESIRE**. Don't miss these unforgettable love stories by some of romance's hottest authors. Silhouette Desire—where your fantasies will always come true....

DES-GEN

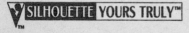